Sex, Lies

&

Dirty Laundry

By: Denecia Green

Acknowledgement

I am deeply grateful to God for the gifts He has allowed this journey to bring into my life. He has blessed me in spite of myself, and I am humbled by His grace.

To my family, thanks for your undying love, support and encouragement to follow my dreams; your kind words and gentle nudges catapulted me to new heights.

Many thanks to Ms. Stacey A Palmer, my editor, for your listening ear and literary suggestions that thickened the plot and made my words come to life. To Jonathan Cooke, you are a talented Web designer and Jamie Barnett, a very skilled photographer. Thank you both for creating such an aesthetically pleasing cover.

To my readers, thank you so much for the never ending support you have shown me. You could have done many other things with your hard earned dollars; I am appreciative that you chose to purchase this book; and I hope that you enjoy it.

Also by

Denecia Green

Life: Through A Teen's Eyes

A compilation of short stories capturing the life of typical modern teenagers from various socioeconomic backgrounds. The range of stories cover light hearted experiences such as the first kiss, the power of generosity as well as more heavy set experiences, including dealing with death, abuse and drug addiction. The stories are intended to inspire and guide readers on how to deal with a few challenges of life.

Lies, Sex & Betrayal

In weaving a tapestry of Jamaican life predicted on a get-rich - quick scheme and illegal drug use. Lies, Sex & Betrayal offers an inside look of life on the wild side with chilling intimacy. Kim, the dollar-hungry entrepreneur with her raging thirst for sex, handled her business by any means necessary after her lover; a drug kingpin was placed behind bars. Briana whose main foci were her man and success, was shocked out of her comfort zone after meeting Alex. Both women were forced to face their secret and desires. Lies, Sex & Betrayal is a steamy story with all the plot twists one craves in matters of the heart.

Love, Lies & Temptation (Sequel to Lies, Sex & Betrayal)

Briana and Kim are best friends in their early twenties struggling to navigate their daily lives. Amidst their desire for carnal pleasures and their drive to achieve professional success lie many temptations designed to veer them off track. The two friends, who have both made major mistakes in their personal lives, find themselves wanting more than what they have.

With many heartbreaks under her belt and a relatively successful career, Briana happens upon love in an unexpected place and from the most unlikely man. Finally, she is settled and happy, and everything could not go any better for her. Kim on the other hand, gives up true love and long term peace of mind for the financial riches she has always yearned. The catch is that she will have to sell her soul to the devil to maintain it. In the end, the only thing the two friends have left in common is their love and devotion to each other, but they end up on opposite ends of the happiness spectrum.

1

It's been two weeks since I had last seen the love of my life. With the sunroof rolled back and windows down, I clocked 150mph down the highway as I tried to arrive on time at the airport. I made sure to wear a denim mini skirt with no panties because I knew he loved when I showed off my smooth legs. The moment I woke this morning, I was slapped with horniness in anticipation of my husband's arrival. Fifteen minutes later, I pulled up in the arrival section, just in time to see the sexiest man alive strolling out of the arrival gates of the airport. I exited the vehicle and hugged him tightly... "I missed you so much." I whispered in his ear.

"I missed you too hun," he said while simultaneously caressing and squeezing my ass and with a look of pleasure in his eyes.

I smiled, pulled away from him then walked back toward the vehicle. "Are you wearing undies?," he asked as he closed the door.

"Nope" I responded, driving off. He leaned over and kissed me on the neck while slowly caressing my thighs. He slid his hands further under my skirt, caressing my clit. My juices start flowing immediately. It didn't take much for him to turn me on, and I know this was one of the things he loved about me since he loved sex as much as I did.

I moaned. "Baby stop; you are distracting me. You might make me have an accident."

"Relax baby and keep your eyes on the road."

Honestly, who was I kidding? I didn't want him to stop. It felt so good, so I opened my legs wider, moaning as he slipped his fingers into my pussy.

"Yes baby, you are already nice and wet, just the way I like it."

"Oh Gossshhhh," I moaned, swerving on the other side of the highway. "Babe, if you keep doing this, you are going to make me cum."

"Sounds good to me…Cum all over my fingers or pullover and let me put this hard ass dick in you."

I looked at him contemplating the latter option for a split second but opt to enjoy the finger fuck instead. He placed another finger in, this time hitting a spot. I swerved again. "Ahhhh…shit." I pressed down on the accelerator. I think I was now hitting a 100mph. He pumped his fingers even harder into my wetness while using his thumb to flick my clit. I started to shake, clutching the steering wheel. "Oh shitt….I'm cumin." I screamed and zig zagged in and out of traffic as I nut all over his fingers. He pulled out his hands and placed his sticky fingers in my mouth. "Damn, I taste so good." Eating those pineapples has really paid off. I slurped up my own juices. I smiled, reached over and rubbed his bulge. God I loved this man.

****

I met Michael over 6 years ago at The Renaissance hotel. I was sitting alone, totally engrossed in my battered shrimp and a glass of white wine when I heard a voice speaking the Queen's English.

"I hope you are enjoying your appetizer?"

I looked up at a pair of the warmest pale blue eyes, I had ever seen. They hypnotized me from the first moment I made contact.

"I am sorry. My name is Michael Sharpalova, and I am the owner of this restaurant. Your meal is on me tonight."

From that quaint meeting, we began dating. It wasn't rushed; it was almost like a natural progression. I wasn't sure why I felt the way I did around him. I had an increasingly warm reaction towards him from the moment I met him. He was barely cute. I have had numerous men approach me in the past who were far better looking than he was, and I wouldn't give them the time of day but Michael was different. He was kind, respectful and had a welcoming spirit; qualities that all the other men lacked. He was old fashioned about dating, and this suited me very well. I thoroughly enjoyed the slow non-threatening pace of our relationship. It was 3 months of dating before he attempted to kiss me. The men I dated always tried to do that on the first date. With Michael, on the other hand, heavy petting didn't enter the picture until about 7 months after we met. I was comfortable with him leading the way into the intimate aspects of our relationship. I was in love with him from the beginning. His personality won my heart.

At the time we met, he was 35, and I was 24. He is the owner of about 10 restaurants, several properties in Jamaica and Florida; he is a custom broker and part owner in a car dealership. He was a multi-millionaire who took great care of his family. His sisters and a few relatives were now in college thanks to his financial support. I was so pleased with his devotion to family, especially his mother. She wasn't short of anything, and he scheduled quality time with her every week.

He loved traveling to French Polynesia. It was one of his favorite things to do, so the day he invited me to travel with him to Tahiti, I was elated. It was an awesome vacation for both of us. One day we boarded a private yacht for lunch, when he proposed. Of course, I accepted. I was beside myself with joy. The crew completely pampered us. We sailed to various locations where he showered me with gifts. We got couples massage, snorkeled, scuba dive, participated in motorized sports, visited the Faarumai waterfall and ate shrimp, lobster, caviar and champagne until we grew weary but it was a breathtaking vacation. It was more than romantic; at times I felt like I was living a dream.

We enjoyed every moment with each other in the beginning of our union. Michael was open to a lot of things, and he believed that we both should experience the full carnal pleasures of life. I was willing to please my man, so I agreed to just about anything he wanted. We devoured illustrated sex manuals, viewed sexually explicit tapes, and I would try to compete with the stars. I even went out of my way to purchase a countless amount of sex toys.

After a year of experiencing all the sexual positions from the Kama Sutra, using all type of dildos, vibrators, anal plug, gag ball, sex swing, oils, sensual massages as well as engaging in a few menage a trois, I became a fully sexually aware, multi-orgasmic woman. Michael had successfully activated his wife's freak button.

This led me to create a special room in the house; I called it the *torture room*. I installed a pole and watched myriad's of videos on YouTube on how to use it until I became a pro. Michael was never bored. In fact, he slowly realized that he had created a monster. I wanted sex all the time and so did he. We were the perfect couple

2

After 4 years of marital bliss and a stable career, I yearned for a child. Although Michael agreed I, unfortunately, had difficulties getting pregnant. I had not taken contraceptive in about one year and still nothing happened, so we both decided to get a thorough medical check. We received an infertility evaluation and we were presented with the options of taking fertility drugs, intrauterine insemination and in vitro fertilization.

Intrauterine insemination involves a healthy sperm being placed directly in the uterus around the time of ovulation whereas in vitro fertilization involves stimulating and retrieving multiple mature eggs from a woman, fertilizing them with a man's sperm in a dish in a lab, and implanting the embryos in the uterus three to five days after fertilization. After extensive research about the cost and complications of these procedure and a heart to heart talk with Michael, I added adoption in the mix. He immediately dismissed the adoption proposal and insisted that taking the medication seemed like a more suitable option.

I began my regimen with Clomiphene 50mg once daily for five days starting on the 3rd day of my menses. After the first cycle, my dose was increased to 100mg once daily for five days then to 150mg. Despite my efforts, all three attempts were unsuccessful. Disappointed and a bit upset with myself about my infertility issue, I became emotionally stressed. Though he never said or showed it, I convinced myself that Michael became disappointed with our marriage. He channeled his energies into expanding his restaurants into other cities and purchasing properties in other countries. He was still carving his niche, and I was proud of him, but I found myself feeling sad and lonely. With more assets, came more traveling, longer meetings and business trips for Michael, and I found myself unintentionally bitching constantly. The sex slowly disappeared from our marriage, and his response to that issue was that "the frequency of sex naturally declines with old married couples." I was not even sure what he meant because I was nowhere near elderly; I was still in my twenties. I supposed this was the repercussion of my inability to conceive. However, I was still hornier than ever, so I put my dildos to work and gave Michael a break. Of course gadgets cannot be compared to the real deal, but it would have to suffice.

We were experiencing a slow month at my office, so I had a lot of free time on my hands. I decided to take more interest in his businesses, assisting in whatever way I could. Michael supported my efforts and found a good partner in me but he still travelled often and left me behind most times. So the sadness would prevail once more. On a few occasions, he would take me with him but this was no different as he left me alone at the hotel to attend his meetings. This wasn't new to me but everything started to become a nuisance of late... I decided that maybe both of us needed to get away for a few days. I tried to lure him away for a vacation, but he declined. I guess he sensed my disappointment so he suggested sending me to one of my favourite places for a week; Punta Cana.

"You deserve a break honey. You should go without me and unwind. I know you will enjoy it because you love it there."

This was true. There was never a dull moment whenever I vacationed in Punta Cana. The luxurious hotels, the beaches, the various tours allowing you to bask in and appreciate the ambience of such a beautiful country. Even though I was not at all happy with his decision, I still agreed to the trip. Maybe it will revitalize my whole well-being.

****

Once there, the first thing I scheduled was a spa day. My treatment consisted of a water massage with warm stones, a refresher facial, manicure and a pedicure. I was totally at ease. The only distraction was the buff sexy men catering to my needs. Some were quite brazen and willing to provide more than the spa treatment. As much as I yearned good sex, I ignored their advances. I was after all, a one man woman. I belonged to Michael and to him only. I enrolled in their daily regimen of activities; I did everything from water sports to yoga, ballroom dancing to karaoke. You name it, I was a part of it. As the days went by, I participated in a few tours in and around Santo Domingo and of course their night life. There was no way I could vacation in Punta Cana and not visit *Imagine Night Club*. I was enjoying my vacation. I felt like a new woman. I was refreshed and ready to go back home to my husband. Especially because my hormones seemed to have gone haywire for the entire trip. The moisture brewing between my legs became more intense with the passing of time. I swear if I even breathed too deeply, I became turned on.

Just my luck, my neighbours decided to have really loud, hardcore sex that woke me up in the wee hours of the morning. The moans and the dirty talk were so loud and clear, I had to open my door to see if they were actually in the hallway. I couldn't believe I was hearing every breath, every grunt, and every smack on the ass from my room. I was thoroughly turned on.

I closed the door and grabbed my pink electronic bunny, laid on the floor, spread my legs and caressed my pussy. The more she moaned, the more turned on I became. Every

14

thrust that I heard, I shoved my toy deeper in my wet pussy. And as her moans quickened, so did my speed of penetrating my pussy. I grabbed my breast with one hand and thrust the toy further and deeper into my pussy with the other hand. I was writhing on the floor, as my neighbours took me to new heights. When she screamed out "harder baby", I was moaning even more as my body prepared for the explosion that was about to happen. By this time, my bunny was penetrating my moisture at lightning speed. We both screamed in unison as I released the best orgasm since I had been in Punta Cana. I went back in the bed feeling, renewed. As I waited for sleep, my neighbours resumed with round 2 about 20 minutes later and so did I. That night turned out to be beautifully orgasmic.

3

I couldn't wait to fuck my husband. After what I encountered the night before, I was ready for the real deal, so I took the first flight out the next day. I was going to surprise Michael and hopefully have a little fun in the torture room before he left for work. As we pulled into the driveway, I felt relieved seeing the vehicle. That meant that everything will go as planned. The driver brought my luggage and set them down in the foyer. I tipped him generously, and he left. Everything was still intact like he hadn't ventured downstairs all morning. I poured myself a glass of water then quietly ventured up the stairs, since I wasn't sure if he was still asleep.   As horny as I was, I didn't want to disturb him, if that were the case. I paused for a second, because I swore I heard a moan. I listened but heard nothing a second time. I think I must have been hung up on the encounter the night before. I made my way to the bedroom but was distracted by voices I heard this time coming from the torture room. "Damn this shit is good and tight," I heard Michael say. By now, I stopped breathing. I heard another moan. I knew for sure, my mind wasn't playing games with me. I approached the room and what I saw, I would not have been prepared to see in a million years. In the sanctuary that I created, I watched my husband ramming his dick into someone's ass. He thrust his steel hardened penis, jackhammer style without remorse. The sound of flesh pounding against his body echoed throughout the room. Torrential sweat poured over his body as he fucked that ass like a stallion. I watched the scene for what seemed like an eternity. I was in shock. All I was able to see, was my husband's lovely, long, rock hard, 9 inches of cock in someone's ass unprotected. They were oblivious to my presence. As his pumping action intensified, his body prepared for the electrical discharge of pleasure that was about to happen. He released his load and ripped his dripping penis out of the person's ass. My husband was totally satisfied with the experience. Thick semen seeped out of the person's anus. That's when I really noticed the individual. He spun his partner around and they engaged in a deep kiss. That's when I gasped.

"Oh fuck," I heard him say. I vomited. When I saw the nicely chiseled body and the dick hanging between my husband's partner" s legs, I vomited even more. My husband was fucking a man, Rambo style, in my sanctuary.

"Get out!!!!" I screamed at the top of my lungs almost on the brink of tears. I watched as he searched for his clothes. I was not about to wait for this nigga to get dressed. "Get the fuck out of my house," I repeated, this time scooping up the vomit and throwing it at the bastard.

"You bitch," he squealed as he dodged the first pile of vomit. I ran towards him angrily and he ran in a circle around the room before heading to the exit, but then he slid in the vomit and fell. I grabbed sculpture piece we bought on our last vacation together. It was the most likely weapon since it fit perfectly into my hands. As I attempted to beat the son of a bitch, Michael grabbed me and allowed him to escape. As I kicked and fought to free myself from his grip, I tried to remember where I stored my gun because Michael, deserved two bullets in his cock. Anger clouded my judgement and I couldn't remember shit. So I slapped him a few times with the sculpture until he released me.

"Ouch, what is wrong with you?" was all he could muster. He sounded stupid as fuck!

"What the fuck is wrong with me? What the fuck is wrong with *you* Motherfucker? You are getting too old to fuck me but you find the time to fuck another man's ass...I hate you." I screamed.

"Honey..." he said approaching me with open arms.

"Don't touch me," I screamed. "Get out" He stood looking at me with amazement.

"Get out!!" I screamed once more, only this time tears escaped. Next thing I knew, my chest tightened, I was gasping for air then the room started spinning, then everything went blurry as my body hit the floor.

4

I woke up in a hospital bed. I looked around and the son of a bitch was fast asleep at the bedside. The ordeal replayed in my mind, and it made me sad once more. I burst out in tears frightening Michael out of his slumber.

"What's wrong Hun?" he asked while approaching the bed.

"Do not touch me!!!" I slapped his hands as he attempted to hug me.

"I love you Joslyn"

"More than you love men?" I asked

"Really, you had to go there?"

"I believe I am just highlighting facts. I mean, after all you pounded that ass like you owned it. Not to mention that explosive orgasm you had, that you haven't gotten with me in Lord knows how long? "

There was an awkward pregnant pause.

"Look, Jos, I am really sorry"

"Sorry about what exactly; that you got caught? Because if I didn't can you imagine how many more men you would have fucked?"

"Can you stop it…It's not like that"

"What is it like Michael, because I am confused?" My voice cracked when I said this. "Have our marriage been a lie? Was it to cover up your gay tendencies because you are a renowned businessman? You must be elated that I can't get pregnant. Did you even want a child?" I fought hard to hold back the tears.

"Yes I want a child. I want to have as many kids as I can afford to have with you. I love you and want to spend the rest of my life with only you. I have a fetish that I satisfy occasionally."

"A fetish?" I asked sarcastically. I wasn't even sure why I was entertaining this level of conversation on the matter.

"Yes a fetish. I love anal sex"

"Let's stop the bullshit right now. We have anal sex and you have never orgasmed during the encounter. So what you have is not a fetish; you are attracted to men, plain and simple."

"No I am not," he protested.

"Or is it that my ass is just not tight and warm enough for you?"

"Omg Jos, can you stop?" he said with a combination of anger and disgust.

"Why do you look so disgusted? It was heights of pleasure moments ago as you watched your semen seep from his ass. So much so, that you had to seal it with a kiss? How long have you been fucking men?"

I am not sure how much, if anything, the nurse heard, but luckily for him her presence interrupted my wrath. She performed her routine checks.

"Mrs. Williams, your blood pressure is still a bit elevated. I need you to try and get some rest soon. I am sure you want to go home to your husband.

"He is the damn stress factor," I mumbled

She laughed. "I will give you both a few more minutes, but I need you to try and rest please?" she begged once more before exiting.

"So how long have you been fucking men?" I jumped right back to the question.

"It's a recent encounter. I felt overwhelmed one night after work when you were away getting one of your fertility shots, and I decided to stop by a bar in the city. I had a few drinks then Eli came by, we had a few more drinks then next thing I know we were kissing then we had sex."

"Had sex at the bar?"

"Yes. There is a little motel that partners with the bar, so he took me there."

"He took you there? And you went casually just like that?" I said trying to fathom his explanation.

"I had quite a few to drink" he responded.

"Were you able to drive home that night?" I asked

quizzically.

Without thought, he responded. "Yes".

"If you were sober enough to drive home that night, then you could have said no to a man who made sexual advances at you. That explanation is unacceptable. But anyway, that was the bar. How did all this fast forward to my torture room?"

"It happened a few times after that."

"A few times?" I interrupted. "So you clearly were enjoying it?"

"I guess?" He was casual in his response – very matter-of-factly and non-chalant.

I felt my stomach churn.

"Is that when you lost interest in me?"

"I didn't lose interest in you. I just became a little stressed when all you talked about was having a baby and then when sex became calculated with your ovulation kit, it was killing the moment for me. Then after your fourth month of treatment and yet another conception failure, you started crying a lot in the midst of sex and I just couldn't handle it anymore."

"So your answer to the issues we were having was to go fuck a man to get over me?"

"I know it may look bad. But it's not something I went searching for; it just happened."

"If it remained as a one off encounter at the club then it would have "just happened" but you invited him back to the house, which is saying I am comfortable with you or is suggestive of some type of long term arrangement. And of all the places, you had to contaminate my torture room; my safe haven?"

"I am so sorry honey...I will stop seeing him. I love you"

"You don't need to stop seeing him. If that is what makes you happy, then go ahead and do you" I said with a smile.   I was already planning my out.

He looked relieved as if he really thought I would have made such a compromise. He must be fucking retarded.

"However, I would like you to sign the divorce papers as soon as they are sent to you."

"I am not signing any divorce papers," he said angrily. Meanwhile I am here wondering why he is even getting upset. Who is the victim here?

"Sign the papers or move out of the house?" I said

"I am not signing any papers. We are in this together until death do us part. You seem to have forgotten the oath we took in the presence of the Lord."

He was that pompous.

"Fuck you!!" I screamed.

"Get out!!" He didn't move.

"Get out...Get out of the room!" I screamed frantically until the nurse came in.

"Mr. Williams, you need to leave. This is not helping her condition right now. She needs to relax, she said politely as she pointed towards the door.

"Please try to remain calm and get some rest," she said once more before exiting the room with Michael.

I cried. This time uncontrollably, because I wasn't sure how to move forward. I can't get over the images in my head. I don't think I can ever forgive him but I love him.

5

After being discharged from the hospital, I pretty much stayed in bed for the rest of the day. I was still trying to come to terms with Mikey being a bisexual. The more I thought about it, the more my headache intensified. I felt betrayed. The incident replayed in my head, and I cringed at the thought of him liking men more than women. If ever there was a time I wished Mikey had cheated on me with a woman, it would have been now. I failed at becoming a mother and now my marriage was headed for a similar fate.

I was emotionally unstable and didn't think I was quite ready to resume my work schedule but staying at home would only result in me feeling even more desolate and bereft.

How does one get over seeing her husband with another man? How was I supposed to move forward? I knew Michael was not about to sign the divorce papers that easily, especially since he opt to move out the house for a little while allowing me space and time to gather my thoughts. I am not sure I had the energy in me to argue to the end either.

I needed a backup plan. I want to hurt his ego and make him suffer. I need him to feel as much hurt as I did, because his response to the ordeal was way too casual. "I am sorry" was not enough for me. I laid on the bed in silence for a few hours.

I felt like this encounter had given me permission to cheat. Why should I still endorse monogamy if the end result was the same? What's the point? Society thinks a woman should be given one dick, and she should be happy with it for the rest of her life. Even if that dick has been in many vaginas, we should turn a blind eye to all that and accept it. On the other hand, it is acceptable for a man to fully indulge and enjoy sex with whomever he wants whenever he wants, but a woman cant? Well I was about to defy that rule. I was about to start enjoying sex with as many different partners as possible. Today was the last of me letting society's narrow scope about what they think you should do with your vagina, determine what you should do with your vagina. I was ready to use this pussy and enjoy it. Fuck, fuck, fuck until you run out of dicks. Travel to other countries and have sex. Explore the full range of everything and feel zero shame. Michael didn't!

With that mindset, I jumped out of bed feeling like I was ready to tackle the world. That was my back up plan. If Michael found out, then he should be more than happy to sign the papers. After all, people like him wouldn't accept anything less than publicly declaring oneself to be in a monogamous relationship. I don't see any reason why this wouldn't work. I gathered a few pieces of clothing and began ironing in preparation for the rest of the work week.

The moment I completed that chore, I was greeted by a delivery at the gate. It was a beautiful floral arrangement containing a mixture of red roses and baby's breath; my favourite. Accompanying that was a box of Ferrero Rocher chocolates accompanied by a note which read: *"I felt so ashamed that I did that to you; you are the best thing that has ever happened to me and I am sorry. Sorry doesn't mean anything when I say it to the world, but it means the world when I say it to you. Please forgive me? I will do whatever it takes to keep you in my arms. I love you Jos. Have a blessed Sunday."*

The floral arrangement was absolutely gorgeous and the note was cute – if he had done something as simple as breaking my favorite vase – but not sufficient for what he did. It meant nothing to me. I was ready to play.

"Let the games begin baby", I said as I walked back to the house with a smirk on my face.

6

Mondays were usually unpredictable because I kept the schedule open. It was the only day I facilitated walk-in clients.

My first client of the day was via telephone. Tiffany, my assistant, told me who it was before transferring the call. George was a client I was introduced to two years ago as I helped him to adjust to life as a single, socially anxious man. He had a hard time getting over his ex-girlfriend, so he tried to cope by going out with multiple women. But a mysterious health scare a few months ago led to us talking every Monday as I supported his navigation through the medical maze.

"The tests came back, and I have cancer which has metastasized," he said. "I probably have a couple of months to live." I felt a piercing pain in my chest instantly. I hated that condition more than anything. Cancer is that one illness that will immediately drain you emotionally and mentally and take you home sooner than the actual illness itself.

"I am so sorry George," was all I could manage to say.

"I will be fine. No man lives forever, and now I know I have limited time left, I will make the most of it."

"George, remember when you mentioned that you didn't want to die alone or without having the chance to love someone again? Is this still a priority for you now?"

"To me, alone means that no one knows me. After two years, I feel known by you. As long as you are around, I'm not alone," he said.

"That's really good to know," I responded. We chit-chatted a little bit, then our conversation ended shortly after.

The mood quickly changed when the first person to burst through the door was Michael. He plopped himself down on the couch and greeted me with, "did you get my package? I know how much you love those?"

"Why are you here?" I was irritated.

"To check on my wife," he said smiling from ear to ear.

If I could smack the smirk off his face, I would. It bothered me that he was so collective and happy.

"Get out!"

"I miss you. I want to come home Jos..." He got up from the couch. That's when I notice the bulge in the front of his pants. I felt my knees buckle instantly and a gush of moisture between my legs.

Oh god, he is so sexy...I fought the urge and held my composure. I eased him off when he attempted to hug me.

"You need to leave," I said sternly.

"When can I come home?"

"As soon as you are ready to sign the divorce papers."

He took a few steps back in disbelief.

"Agreeing to a divorce will be the last thing I do Joslyn," he headed towards the door, pound it angrily before reiterating, "It will be the last thing I do, you hear me!" then he stormed out.

I was so angry. I am glad I had gotten a half hour to cool down before my next client showed up.

****

My next client, Mr. Wesley, was here because the court ordered him to have sessions to help curtail his anger issues which he denies. His ex-girlfriend took out a restraining order against him and he has been having a hard time coping since. What was interesting about Mr. Wesley was that he was a church Deacon, but I often questioned his faith on the premise that he was very comfortable with the double life he lived. I try not to judge, since we all, at some point we will have all fallen short of the glory of God and would have done things that we are not proud of, but when you do these things repeatedly without any form of remorse, I think something is terribly wrong with that. For me, that is an indication that you need a spiritual reassessment. He has made several attempts to kiss me in the past, but what happened later in this session blew me over.

After allowing him to vent about the fact that his exwoman had moved on to another man and seemed happier than when they were both together, he had a major melt down. So I moved over to him and hugged him, and he embraced it. This helped to somewhat calm him down but then when he placed one hand on my legs, things got awkward. I removed his hands and he replaced them. This time, I slapped him and told him to stop but it seemed like that gesture only triggered something inside of him. Next thing I knew, he gripped both my legs firmly, yanked me towards him, knocking me down on the sofa.

So frightened by everything that was happening, I couldn't scream. I laid rigidly on the couch as I tried to process what was really happening. He opened my legs then planted kisses along my inner thighs and made his way up to my sweet spot. That was when I snapped.

"Stop it!!! Stop It Wesley!!" I screamed as I tried to push his head from between my legs. But he became forceful and pushed back. He nipped my underwear with his teeth and I pounded him hard in his head for him to stop. As soon as he did, I jumped off the couch and ran to my desk.

"What the fuck is wrong with you?"

"Just let me taste you baby...Please just let me taste you?" He approached me.

"Mr. Wesley, you are a Christian; matter of fact, you are

a deacon. Why are you acting like this?"

"You are so fucking sexy Joslyn, I can't help it."

"Oh my God, are you hearing yourself? What you are doing is wrong and you need to seriously pray about it because by the look of things, it seems like a regular occurrence. Although I don't go to church, this is against everything that Christianity stands for. What you are doing is not okay. You would have sucked the life out of my vagina if I allowed it then walk out of here unbothered. Its people like you, why people like me hate the church. You can't be telling people to follow Christ then you are out in the world offering free oral sex. You need help!"

I was ranting. I was pissed!

It was as if he couldn't help himself.

"I am sorry...I am really sorry!!" he said before the emotional outburst. He cried uncontrollably, and I stood there speechless. I actually felt sorry for him. I don't think I had ever seen a grown man sob like that before and for a moment, I felt happy about his reaction. I was happy that, I could make him feel badly about his actions, because this was a small indicator that all hope wasn't lost. He sobbed and sobbed. I watched him from a distance, offering no form of comfort this time.

I was trying to decide whether this ordeal warranted a termination of our sessions but then I watched him sob and listened to him apologize about a million times, and immediately felt like he deserved a second chance. So I forgave him. When he finally pulled himself together, he apologized once more before leaving. I had a session with one more client before ending my work day. I felt a bit uneasy, but I think the feeling was mostly that of disappointment with Mr. Wesley. Before this incident, I had a certain level of respect and admiration for him. Now, I wasn't sure what to conclude about him and his ministry. I was disgusted, to say the least.

7

I poured myself a glass of wine the moment I arrived home. I really needed to find some form of extracurricular activity to better manage my stress levels. My stress levels were heightened by the lack of sex, so this was definitely a lethal combination. I took a sip of my wine and reminisced on the day's events, particularly my encounter with Mr. Wesley. For a brief moment I wondered how his tongue would have felt on my clit. The truth is, he was an attractive man.

"Oh God, I am going to hell for even thinking that. What is wrong with me?"

I took another sip of my wine then headed upstairs. I paused at the door of my torture room. I need to have this remodeled, because I don't think I would ever be able to use this room again. I continued to the bedroom, turned on the television and switched to "El Chapo" on Netflix. I plopped myself onto the bed and enjoyed my wine and movie. But for some strange reason, I kept thinking about Mr. Wesley. I am not sure why I became so obsessed with the thought of him giving me oral sex. To make it even worse. It was turning me on the more I thought about it. Now I was totally distracted from "El

Chapo" and more focused on the moisture brewing between my legs. I placed the wine on the night stand, unbuttoned my shirt then fondled my breast. With one hand cupping my breast, I worked the other one down to my vagina, strumming my clit. By this time, my underwear was completely soaked. I paused and went to the drawer for a rag to dry myself. This started off fine but then I realized that the more I rubbed, the more I became aroused. Soon the rag was discarded in favour of my fingers. I leant back against the closet, parted my legs and went to work on my pussy, fantasizing about the deacon's erect cock and what I would do with it. My clit was swollen and in need of attention. I inserted three fingers and gyrated for a few minutes. I thrust them in and out building up to a crescendo. They were working faster and faster flashing in and out. I pictured the deacon in front of me, and I imagined his hands on my hips and his touch on my naked body as he moved closer. I needed more. I needed to be fully penetrated, so I went for my dildo that was neatly stashed in my drawer. This one was one of my favorites because it had about 5 different speeds. I placed it on the third one which also had a twisting motion at the head. I laid on the bed with my legs spread as widely as they could go. I inserted the dildo, closed my eyes and bit my lips as I imagined him pounding my slippery pussy. I moaned at that thought and maxed the speed on my gadget. I writhed in pleasure on the bed, gripping the sheet as I could feel the orgasm nearing. I imagined him pounding me even harder, and I thrusted the dildo further up inside of me at lightning speed.

"Ahhhhh... Yessssss!!!!!" I screamed, lifting my pelvis off the bed, as I squirted juices. I tossed my dildo aside, and laid on the bed with arms and legs spread apart, finally releasing all the built up energy. My thoughts switched from Mr. Wesley to Michael until I felt sleep creeping in.

8

A few hours later, I woke up feeling very sticky and dirty. I headed straight for the shower. I stripped and stood under the hot water for a few minutes. I missed my husband. I craved his touch, his body against mine, the softness of his lips with his kisses and the hardness of his teeth as he bit my lips. I replayed one of our sexual encounters in my mind. I began to imagine his presence, placing my hands on his chest and basking in the memory of how good he felt. I closed my eyes, and tears streamed down my cheeks. I turned off the shower and stepped onto the cold tiles. I wrapped a towel around me and made my way downstairs to pour another glass of wine. I surveyed the kitchen and contemplated moving out of this house, because it was filled with too many memories. A few minutes later, keys were rumbling at the front door. Michael entered and before I could protest, he grabbed me and pushed me against the wall. The glass fell from my hands. He held me by my neck, kissed me on the cheek then whispered "I miss you. You can fight me and scream all you want tonight but I am fucking you." I gasp at the sound of that. I was practically wet. Still pinned to the wall in a choke hold, I heard him unbuckle his pants. He removed the towel, and I quivered as I felt his bare skin against mine.

"You are dripping, literally dripping. You know you want this." I felt my juices running down my inner thigh. He dipped and slid his cock between the cracks of my ass then to the front then to the back, taking care to lubricate his cock with my juices. He then leaned me forward at an angle that was perfect for him to slide fully inside me. I let out a moan at how good that felt. He grabbed my hair and arched my body back to him. My body tightened when he thrust powerfully inside me. He pulled out then reentered even more forcefully. I released another moan of content and pleasure. Still holding my neck and hair, he led me to the island in the kitchen and bent me over. Using this for leverage, I could now take in more of his cock. I could feel him growing inside me. He ravaged my body, and his hard fuck was causing me to lose my balance. He pulled out, then I felt his tongue gliding from my clit to my ass hole. He did that for a few minutes before thrusting in me again. This time, reaching under to grab my breast, massaging and pinching my nipples. This set me off even more. He took my body, stroke by stroke. Everything belonged to him. He smacked me on the ass a few times then shoved his fingers in my ass. My pussy clenched at that surprise and the force of the impact. He was thrusting so hard and fast, I felt my orgasm mounting. I tried to tell him I was coming but the words fall apart before it could leave my mouth. He thrust deeper sending my eyes in the back of my head and the wind from my lungs. My body started to spasm as my orgasm hit. A few seconds later, he orgasmed. I felt his dick spurt long, warm streams over my back and ass. My body sent me into after shock and I collapsed to the floor. He fell next to me and we both laid there in silence panting. Soon after, we regained our breathing and all the spasms halted.

He hugged me, then whispered once more "I miss you Joslyn." I remained silent. I missed him too, but I didn't know what to do. Great sex always impaired my judgement, so I was not about to address the situation in the aftermath of the great sex session. All I knew, was that this moment was everything and this sexual encounter was long overdue. We both drifted to sleep on the kitchen floor.

9

The next morning, I awoke in the warmth of my bed. I must admit, I think that was the best sleep I had gotten since my return from Punta Cana. Last place I remember being was on the kitchen floor. I don't recall him moving me to the room, but I appreciated it. I was also relieved that he left, because I couldn't be bothered with any discussion. I looked at the clock then hopped into the shower. I still had adequate time on my hands before getting dressed for work. I stood under the shower and replayed last night's bliss. I needed to stay focused. If I keep welcoming sex, I am definitely sending mixed signals, and I am pretty steadfast on my decision to divorce him. His encounter with another man marked the end of the road for me. I felt neglected and incomplete as his wife because I was unable to give him a child. I am not sure how we could move past that, especially when I knew how badly he desired children. I took my final spin under the shower before wrapping myself in a towel. I opened the door, only to be greeted with a tray on the bed containing eggs benedict, a granola parfait and orange juice. I thought he left. I sat on the bed and took a bite of my eggs benedict. The sauce he drizzled over the English muffin was everything. I licked my lips at how sumptuous it was. It was exactly what I didn't know that I needed.

"I see you are enjoying breakfast," He entered the room as if he was resolute that we were rekindled.

"Yes, it's delicious. Thank you."

"Anything for you," he said kissing me on the forehead. I watched him lay out his outfit before heading to the shower. I hope this bastard didn't think that last night's encounter was an invitation for him to move back in. I finished my meal then resumed getting ready for work. Moments later he stepped out of the bathroom and my heart leapt. I watched him stroll his sexy ass across the room with his prized possession dangling between his legs. With reflections from the mirror, I kept a close eye on him as he dressed for work.

"You know you are not allowed to sleep here tonight right?" I said breaking the silence. He looked up at me surprised before responding, "Really, after what we shared last night, don't you miss it?"

I didn't answer. "The way you dripped all over the floor, there was no way you could deny that."

"You are not sleeping here!" I said, this time with more force.

"Why are you being so difficult? How long will you punish me for this?"

"I should just move past you shoving your dick inside a

42

man unprotected?"

"You mean the same dick I shoved inside you last night unprotected?"

I gasp at that comeback. Those words burn like hell. I was disgusted, and couldn't believe he just said that.

"Get the fuck out!!!!!" I screamed.

"Babe, I am sorry"

"Get out," I said tossing a pillow at him. I was slowly transforming into Jos the lunatic and he sensed it.

"Alright!!! Alright!!! I am going. Let me just please finish getting dressed and I will be gone."

"You are an idiot," I said before storming out the room.

I finished getting dressed in another room and didn't calm down until I heard him go out the front door.

"Son of a bitch," I murmured. I left for work a few minutes later, still having adequate time.

****

I arrived on time, chatted a bit with my assistant then browsed through the newspapers. My first client for the day, seemed to have a sexuality issue. He had multiple anal encounters with men and became so sexually aroused by them that he was now wondering if he was gay or a bisexual. What are the odds that I had to be the one to get a case like this on a day like today? I felt like I was being tested or like someone was playing a cruel joke on me. I didn't even know how to address the issue.

"Do you still get turned on by women?"

"Yes," he answered. "And I still enjoyed sex with my girlfriend, but I thoroughly enjoyed penetrating a man's ass, more than my girlfriend's vagina."

"Well then," I thought.

"Have you ever had anal sex with your girlfriend?"

"Hell no, she would never let me do that but I love it so much. I am not sure I can live without doing it." He was concerned that he might be more gay than he was bisexual.

"I wouldn't be so quick to put titles on it as to whether you are gay or not until at least attempting anal sex with your girlfriend. Both of you need to discuss the issue in its entirety. I prefer this method but then because women can be very firm on their decisions. You need to get her to try it.

Firstly, you need to ensure that her mind and body are completely relaxed in order for her to feel pleasure instead of pain. Secondly, find a comfortable position. She shouldn't have to worry about holding the position. Choose one that allows easier access, doggy style is a good option. You may also put pillows underneath her so she can just lay there and relax.

"I feel like I should be making notes," he said.

"You can, but I am pretty sure you will remember everything I am saying. Its sex we are talking about." We both laughed.

I continued, "Next pointer is to ensure that you use lubricant before any type of anal play; preferably one that is water or silicone-based, because it won't break the condom. Put lots of lubricant in her anus, on your fingers, sex toys, whatever gadget you may be using. Next step is to relax her butt area with your fingers. Caress, kiss and massage her butt then slowly start using your fingers. You may start with the pinky. Go very slowly and gently giving her time to get used to the sensation. Then you may switch to your ring finger then your middle finger, dependent on how she reacts to your pinky. It is very important for you to pay attention to her reactions. If she says, it hurts, then stop and try another time. But if she can handle your fingers then you have hit the jackpot.

"So what happens when I am about to insert my penis?"

"I thought you had that part covered. Didn't you say you have done it and enjoyed it?"

"Yes I have but with experienced people. I didn't need to worry about foreplay, lubricant and all the things you just shared. I penetrate rapidly until I nut."

"Ok well...Seeing that this is her first attempt, nothing will be done rapidly. You will slide the tip of your penis in slowly, remain still and give her time to get used to the sensation of having something bigger in her anus. You will feel the ring of her muscles around the anus tighten and relax. Don't move your penis just let the muscles work. As she relaxes, put an inch further each time. Once again, gage her reaction. Stop whenever she needs to. Always remember to go at her pace until she says she wants more. I think I covered everything." I said as I tapped the pen on my desk, quickly trying to skim through my previous points.

"Oh, how could I forget? I am sure you know this but I am telling you anyway. Remember to never switch from her anus to her vagina because you could spread bacteria and give your partner vaginal infections. If a condom is being used, replace it with a new one before penetrating her vagina. If you are not using one, then wash your penis thoroughly with soap and water before switching to the vagina. Same principle should be applied to using toys and fingers in the vagina after use in the anus. Now that definitely concludes our session on how to perform anal sex, the right way!"

"And I swore you just turned me on. I will definitely put your tips to use"

"After all that, you better! But may I ask what is it about anal sex, why you love it that much; even more than vaginal?" He didn't know this, but I was asking as research for my own situation.

"Anal sex is tighter, more slippery and more pleasurable. I view it as a social accomplishment. When you get a female to do it, it's like a level of sexual prowess that figures significantly into my confidence. I have a sense of dominance and control towards my partner. Simply put, it's just some next level shit."

"We both laughed"

My final question to you "is she aware of your escapades with men?"

"Hell fucking no!! I don't plan to tell her either, so don't even suggest that."

"I would never tell you to do that," I said laughing.

I was just low key hoping the answer was a yes, so I could have gotten a second opinion on such a sensitive matter, I thought.

"Doc, do you love anal sex?"

"That, my friend, is not your business. Remember this session is all about you, so if there are no further issues, I believe that's it for us today?"

"Yes maam," he said dismissing the matter.

"Well enjoy the rest of the day, and I will see you next week," I said as I shook his hand.

As he closed the door behind him, I thought about my similar issue. I shook my head. All he needed to do was to sign the darn papers so I could be happy again.

Twenty minutes later, my next client entered. Two women with two magnificent bodies. One had prominent nipples that were very hard, and left nothing to the imagination in top she wore. The other had beautiful brown eyes and a very warm smile. The one with the hard nipples also captivated me as she made her way to the couch. She had shapely legs, and I watched as her calf muscles flex in her heels. Her figure was a perfect hour glass from her breast down to her waist. While the one with the gorgeous smile, had a perfectly shaped ass.

"How may I assist you ladies today" I said when I believed they were both settled.

"Well its more for my friend, I am just here for support," responded the one with the nice smile. With that said, I focused my energy on Miss hard nipples.

"What's on your mind?"

"I slept with my boyfriend's best friend after finding out he cheated on me. But we have been working things out, and now I am consumed by guilt wondering if I should say something to him. Sometimes I can't help but wonder what would happen if his best friend accidentally blurted it out one day. But then that situation was miniature compared to my other issue." The friend looked at her surprised.

"What other issue is there."

She seemed a little on edge as she shifted in the couch.

"I slept with someone else last night."

"What? How? When...We were together last night?"

I remained silent and allowed the friend to ask her questions.

"I slept with his father?"

"What...Omg... You little bitch!!!"

I was shocked myself.

"When exactly did that happen? Where was I?"

"You were fast asleep. He came by to leave something for him and being intoxicated, I felt a little adventurous so I seduced him. He resisted initially but then gave in."

"I can't believe you. So how was it? Was his cock huge?"

"Umm ladies," I intervened. "Let's stay focused." The friend apologized but then glanced over at her friend with a smile.

"It was so good. He fucked me with both his thumb and his cock. Thumb in my ass and cock in my pussy."

"Shit!!" the friend exclaimed.

"Ladies, let's not do this." I intervened once more, but they ignored me.

"He maintained perfect rhythm as he fucked both my holes hard and fast."

"Bitch you are turning me on."

"Yeah...how much?"

These ladies continued their banter, as if I was invisible and I became captivated by the story so I remained quiet. But then the situation went from 0-100 real quick. Miss hard nipples let her hands venture beneath her friend's skirt as they kissed intensely. I felt my body slightly being aroused by this. The friend let out a moan and I knew for sure her fingers had penetrated her. I felt a gush of moisture between my legs. They fell backward on the couch and held each other as the kissing intensified. Miss nipples removed her fingers, pulled up her friend's skirt, parted her friend's legs then began rubbing her pussy against hers. By this time, I was completely turned on. I watched carefully and as they both started moaning, the more I became aroused. But then things took a turn. They both paused then focused on me. The next thing I knew, they were approaching me.

"You are enjoying this aren't you?" nipples said. The other woman with the perfectly shaped ass spun my chair towards her, grabbed my breast and massaged them. I was so aroused, my boobs were now prominent like Miss Nipples. Nipples made her way around and in a swift motion, shoved her hands between my legs. It was that instant that I regained my senses. "Stop this," I said firmly and shoved them both to the floor.

"What's wrong sweetie? I thought you liked it?" Nipples

said while attempting to regain her composure. They both stood and approached me once more.

"If you touch me again, I will have you arrested" I said.

"We will leave...but can I have your number? Nipples said

"Get out!!" I responded.

"Get out and never come back to this office."

"You are so sexy when you are angry..." her friend said.

I shot her an evil glare.

"Alright, we are leaving."

They brushed their clothes off and headed for the door. The moment they left, my assistant walked in asking if everything was ok. She thought she heard me yell. I reassured her that all was well. I gathered my thoughts and managed to see my last two clients for the day.

****

"What a day!!!" I sighed pulling into my driveway. All I could think about was kicking off my 5 inch heels, stripping off my clothes and lazing in a warm bath. I entered my home and stopped at my favourite part in the kitchen retrieving a bottle of white wine and a glass. I went upstairs, placed the bottle and glass at the side of the bath before preparing it. I returned to the room, where I unbuttoned my blouse and let it fall.

Reaching around, I unsnapped my bra. "Oh that felt so good to have my breasts freed." I briefly massaged my breasts before unzipping my pencil skirt and stepping out of it. I slid my thong off then returned to the bathroom. I ran the water, making sure the temperature was just right before stepping in. I picked up my glass and eased my body in the bath and reminisced about the day. Weirdly, the thing that stood out for me was the encounter with Nipples. As I thought about their touch, I moved my hands over my body. I gently massaged one breast while occasionally pinching and rolling the nipple. After a few minutes of nipple play, my body as alight and ready for more action. I put down the glass and slipped two fingers deep inside my pussy, plunging in and out with rapidly growing urgency. I moaned then grabbed my dildo that was already suctioned to the wall of the tub. I pushed the dildo in and out of my sopping tunnel while using the other hand to make hard circles on my clit. I raised off the bottom of the tub, gyrating and thrusting my hips above the water level. I imagined it was the cock of my husband as I thrust deeper. I felt the orgasm coming. I pumped even faster, holding the side of the tub, to keep my balance, I screamed as I released the juices. I let the dildo slip out of my hand and laid back with a contented smile on my face. I resumed sipping my wine. My mind and body were totally satisfied.

10

Maybe I should forgive him. He said it didn't happen often. He also said that it was something new, and he seemed genuinely sorry about it. To add to that, I really missed him. I can't walk away from four years of marriage because of one mistake. Michael was not known to have affairs either; at least not to my knowledge. I think we should at least have a proper conversation about the ordeal. I had no idea that I was pushing him away indirectly. All this time, I was being hard on myself because I felt embarrassed about my inability to conceive, totally ignoring his feelings.

With all this in mind, I decided to reach out to him via text message, and it went well. Our conversations flowed smoothly for the entire day for the most part. He mentioned the possibility of working late that night to sort paper work. I stopped home after work, freshened up then headed out to purchase something for him to eat. Since he had a long night ahead, I was certain he could use a warm meal.

I called him as soon as I headed his direction, but it went unanswered. I wondered if he had changed his mind and left earlier than he anticipated. I called once more, but still no answer. I arrived at the office and realized that his vehicle was still parked, so I used my spare keys to let myself in.

As I approached the door of his office, I heard familiar sounds. My legs buckled at the thought of reliving the ordeal. Call me paranoid, but I swore the voice, the breathing and every damn thing sounded the same. This cannot be happening again, I thought. What are the odds of me catching my husband again with another man in the space of a few weeks? If this was really happening, it was truly a sign that I should leave this man alone. My hands shook vigorously, almost spilling the food out of the bag. I creeped up to the door and held my breath with tears streaming down my cheeks as I peeked in. Michael had been seated with his head thrown back on his chair with eyes closed. I quickly surveyed the office and no one was in sight; I was so relieved, I headed to the restroom shortly after, where I spent a few minutes trying to regain composure; nerves had gotten the best of me. I washed my face, took couple deep breaths and tried my best to relax. Several minutes later, I approached his office a second time, this time feeling more like myself. Unfortunately for me, my initial thoughts were accurate.

With a completely bare lower body, widened kneeling stance and a fully erect dick, Eli sucked hard, in and out. He looked Mikey in the eye and whisked his shirt up and off, tossing it across the room. He was now totally nude. His hands roamed up his body as he fellated my husband with renewed vigor. I didn't know how to react. I felt nasty watching but Mikey interacted so sensuously with Eli. Eli then tweaked and pinched his erect nipples and to my surprise, he seemed to like it. He allowed Eli to have his way with him until they were ready to switch roles. Eli stood up, and I watched as Michael parted his lips, then darted his tongue out to lick the underside of his cock. He engulfed everything, nibbled then sucked it. I couldn't watch anymore but I got the answer I was looking for. I left the office flooded with emotions I couldn't explain. I must have spent about one hour crying in the parking lot. What was my husband trying to do to me?

In between sobs, I ate the meal I bought for him and kept an eye on the premises, but still there was no sign of Eli leaving. Even so, I had no plans; no end game if I had seen him and Eli leaving together, so what was the point of me staying? I cried some more before I decided to drive my pathetic ass home. My husband had a great deal of dirty laundry.

****

This was some bullshit that I was enduring, and I was enraged. I had so many emotions going on. I was confused. I was hurt. I was angry. I couldn't tell anyone. Surely, it was no one's business what I was going through; the world didn't need to know. I rolled up to work in the Benz like everything was all good. I looked in the rare view mirror and fixed my make-up. "Get it together Joslyn, get it together," I shouted at myself several times.

With the most perfect fake smile, I sauntered into the office and initiated small talk with my staff for a little while, like I usually do, before heading to my office. Today's schedule was light, as I only had two patients confirmed for the morning session, which of course worked in my favour since I wasn't in the best of moods.

Unfortunately, my first client cancelled and that threw me off slightly. I now wished the second client would also cancel, so I could just go home and drown myself in my sorrows. Shortly after my old friend "fucked up luck" decided to pay me a visit. He greeted me with a kiss on the cheek that made my skin crawl.

"Hi honey, how are you? I am sorry I missed your calls last night. I must have been out cold."

Out cold huh, I thought.

"I thought you were working late at the office?"

"That was the plan but then I felt so drained, I had to call it an early night."

Fucking amazing. His responses were just as smooth as his body language. There was no telling he was lying. I was officially concerned. I could only imagine how many times he had probably lied to me in the past and I soaked up everything.

"Well you seem rested and ready to attack today's schedule," was all I could manage to say.

"Yes indeed. I slept beautifully," he said smiling.

"I bet you did."

"You know you can sleep as comfortably as I do if you just allow me to take care of you?"

Unsure as to whether he expected a response to what he said, I ignored the question. He approached my chair, sat on my desk, made eye contact with the warmest pair of coloured eyes.

"Just let me come home. I miss you. I will take care of you like old times."

I decided to break the ice....

"When last have you spoken to Eli?" He looked surprised by the question. The look on his face suggested that he was carefully thinking about his response.

"Not since the ordeal. I realized how upset you were, and I really want to mend our relationship" he said. And just like that, once again, he lied effortlessly. I looked at him with a half-smile before saying "I always had my insecurities but for you to look me dead in the eye and lie so easily without the least bit of remorse, I don't think I can ever trust you again."

"Is this really how things will be between us? You are going to second guess everything I say? I know I hurt you, but you have to try and trust me again?" he said with pleading eyes.

"Try to trust you again?" I repeated

"Yes. It is the only way we can get through this."

"Please tell me how I trust the man who's supposed to be my husband receiving and giving a blow job to another man. The very man you claimed to have last seen weeks ago when I first saw you fucking in our home. That is bad enough, but the fact that you were comfortable enough to carry out the act in our home, and again in your office say a lot. And to think I was considering taking you back. Yet, there you are again with your effortless lies. You were so drained, you called it an early night. No... I am sorry, I mean you were out cold, right?" I put everything out on the table.

An awkward pause permeated the room. I could tell by his lack of response that he felt trapped, shocked and exposed. I am not sure how he managed to not keel over having stopped breathing for such a long time. He looked away from me. When the silence became deafening, he got up and made his way to the door to leave.

He was busted. There was no coming back from the lies he told me. The hurt and the disappointment resurfaced once more.

I decided not to let it affect me, at least temporarily, so I proceeded with my day but "fucked up luck" evil twin "bad luck" decided to pay me a visit.

"Please just hear me out?" he blurted out as he paused at the door.

"Come in and close the door," I said.

"I am really sorry about what happened in our last session. You are a very attractive woman and I can't help the fact that I like every ounce of you. However, I should have never let my desires escape, and for that I am truly sorry. Please do not cancel our sessions. I heard you are one of the better persons to work with and I would love to continue to do so."

For some strange reason, the devil landed on my shoulders, and he was winning. As the deacon apologized, all I could imagine was his lips on my clit. I was about to cross the invisible client/therapist boundary, and I somehow didn't care one bit. I went over and bolted the door, brushed my hands on his leg as I made my way to the sofa. I pulled up my dress then threw one leg over the back arm rest of the couch, giving him full view of my prized possession. After seeing my husband fuck a man for the second time, it's only fair for me to fuck someone else too. I could see the bulge in his pants and that was the confirmation I needed.

Mr. Wesley wasted no time. He got on his knees then licked my inner thighs gently before making his way towards my pussy. He rapidly wiggled his tongue from side to side then flap it up and down against my clit before sliding it in. I arched my back and clutched the couch. "Mmmm!!!!" I tried to keep my moans as low as possible. I squirmed and thrusted my hips the moment he stuck his tongue between the crevices of my pussy, leaving no part of its fleshiness untouched. My breath quickened and I thrashed my head from side to side. I held his head and applied a bit of pressure. He changed the pressure of his tongue on my clit. He went from light feathery tongue strokes, to heavy deep tongue strokes. He alternated from short tongue strokes to fast strokes. He used the front, the side and every angle of his tongue. He slurped, sucked and swallowed even harder. He was giving me different sensations with his diversified technique. He stroked me with his tongue pointed out then curled at the clit to focus on one spot, then flattened it to stroke the full area. He zig-zagged his tongue licking back and forth then swirled it all around my pussy. I could feel my orgasm mounting. This deacon was sucking the hell out of my pussy. In my head, I said this would have happened only once, but I didn't know it would have been this good. I think I will need another dose. I was too close to coming, and I didn't want it to be that quick but he wouldn't slow down. It was blowing my mind. "Ahhhhh...oh god, I moaned" I sent up a prayer for help and immediately felt like a heathen. I rarely prayed and the one time I did, I was asking the good Lord to delay my orgasm. An orgasm being caused by one of "his disciples."

His left hand wandered over my body, squeezing and kneading my breast. With his right hand, he slipped two fingers into my bubbling pussy as if he was searching for Lord knows what. He continued to massage and stroke it. I was becoming desperate and my orgasm was surely coming. It would take divine intervention to stop it. "Oh Lord Jesus help me." He looked up at me, sucked, slurped and licked the fuck out of my fat, juicy ass pussy even more. On some real shit, this Christian nigga sure knew how to eat pussy. When he slipped a finger in my ass, while sucking, that was it. My fountain overflowed in his mouth. I lifted my hips and my body shook intensely. I kept my eyes closed as I tried to recompose myself. When my body finally stopped shaking, I slowly opened my eyes and looked down at him. He was licking his pussy stained lips and grinning.

"You loved that shit didn't you?" I could tell he was proud of himself.

I couldn't even answer because I was in a bit of a daze.
"You want me to fuck you now?"
With no concerns about where I was, I quickly nodded and watched him searched his pockets. He pulled out a condom, dropped his pants then rolled it on. I didn't question why he was walking around with a condom, but I was happy he did-Plus, in our last session we established that he was riding that

train to hell.

I spread my legs wide then he climbed over me. He took my left breast in his mouth and sucked them both alternately like it was a marathon. He swirled his tongue over and around my nipples then placed soft kisses up and down my neck. I moaned. He lifted my legs over his shoulder then pushed the head of the dick into my slippery slit, stretching the mouth of my pussy. I gasp then let out a series of moans as he pumped the dick high inside of me. This shit felt so good. My eyes rolled up in the back of my head as he fucked the shit out me. I grabbed a cushion and buried my face in it, because my moans were getting louder. I loved this dick. He pounded me rigorously until I orgasmed once again and at the same time he did.

I pushed him off me and ran to the restroom because I had to pee urgently. I fixed my hair and clothes and tried to look professional again. When I came out, Mr. Wesley was dressed and ready to leave. I was relieved that he seemed to be following protocol without me having to say it. If he kept this up, we shall get along just fine.

"I enjoyed today's session. Same time next week?" he said extending his arm, and I shook it. The devil sure knew how to prepare a package.

11

Michael and I had still not conversed since our office confrontation. Today marked one week since he was served with the divorce papers and still no word from him. I also felt a little uneasy today because, it was my first time at a business conference without him. As I was leaning down to sign in, I noticed a tattooed arm, a very defined tattooed arm signing in next to me. Intrigued, I looked up at the same time he looked over at me and smiled.

"Good Morning gorgeous," he said confidently. The only thing I managed to do was smile. I am dumb-founded... Finished with registering, he wandered off leaving me there to complete my registration.

As luck would have it, I was seated at the table with several of Michael's colleagues and of course they all questioned me about him.

"It's so weird not seeing you both together. Who would have thought you were separable?" one woman uttered with her unevenly shaped brows.

"Bitch how about you mind your business," I thought to myself, but in reality I smiled and said "I guess we are." Honestly, I had no idea whether or not he would have attended the conference.

About 4 hours into the conference, I decided to skip the next session because I was no longer retaining information. I wandered along the property and discovered a mini bar where I stayed for a bit.

"Trying to turn up at a conference?" I heard a voice say to me from behind. I turned and noticed the guy talking to me was the guy with the tatted arm from the registration table.

"Nah... Just an extended lunch break. I am saturated with information."

"By the way, I am Orlando," he said extending his arm.

"I am Joslyn," I replied.

We chilled at the bar for a while, and we both ended up ordering alcoholic beverages. I enjoyed his company. At one point, I caught miss uneven brows from the conference spying on us but I didn't care. After a few hours of conversation and drinks which flew by, we noticed the conference participants leaving. As we continued to drink, I continued to open up about my husband and I not being on good terms.

"Mmmmm, you seem like a good woman, and I am sorry you are going through that but as much as I enjoyed your company, you are not my type."

A little taken aback by the statement, I questioned why he would make such a bold statement.

"You are nice woman….too nice, which makes you not my type," he said.

Still dumbstruck, I stared at him.

"Let me ask you this. Have you ever had a one night stand or participated in drunk sex or done anything wild?"

I remained silent.

"Exactly, you can't handle me!! I would break you. No offense."

"You don't know me. I am not fragile. You need to stop being so cocky."

Orlando laughed out loud before asking if I was willing to prove it.

"Try me!!" I panned.

"Fine... I have a room here. Its 309. Remember if at any point you want to back out, you are free to do so, and we are good." He said before slapping down money on the counter to cover the bill.

He smiled at me and walked off. Why the hell was he so conceited? A part of me was intrigued by his apparent confidence, so I thought about the offer as I sipped my vodka and cranberry. There was just something about his conceitedness that made me want to prove him wrong. What could he possibly do that I have not done before? I felt butterflies in my stomach. Was about to fuck a random dude I just met? Could I really go through with this? I took a shot of tequila then made my way to the lobby. I slowly meandered to the elevator and pressed the number 3.

When I arrived on the third floor, I paused for a minute, although it seemed like ten, to ponder for a moment on my life and the choices that I have been making of late. Why should I care though? After all, my marriage was over. Everything about the life I thought I had was a façade. I need to enjoy life as it came, however it did. I quickly pushed any doubt I had to the side and proceeded toward his room.

As I walked up to his door, I felt a lump in my throat. I took a deep breath before I lightly knocked. He opened it quickly with a large smile. He was expecting me; I could tell. He motioned for me to come in, and I sauntered past him. He closed the door then pushed me onto the wall, kissing me aggressively. I melted in his arms, embracing his desire with my own. He placed his hands at the sides of my dress, lifting it up so his hands could roam over my ass, gripping it with authority. I loved it. Breaking from the kiss, he looked down at my cleavage and smiled. "I want to see everything." He unhooked my bra and removed it. In a jiffy, he completely undressed me. For some strange reason, I felt completely vulnerable and exposed, so I cupped my breasts to cover them. I felt a little shy. He removed my hands then used his to cup my breasts from underneath, pushing them together. Lowering his head to them, he slowly circled my right nipple with his tongue then my left nipple making them harden. I gasped with pleasure as he continued to flick his tongue along my nipples. He then alternated pulsing on them with increased suction. He stopped and loosed his jeans and lowered them then removed his shirt. Wearing just his boxers, he was stunning. His frame clearly signified that he worked out regularly, as his chest, abs, shoulders and arms were perfectly defined and evenly proportioned. But then my attention was really drawn to his boxers once more. I couldn't understand the curvature that I was seeing. He met my gaze then said "ready?"

"Yes," I replied then he whipped it out. "Holy fuck!!" I thought. This nigga cannot be human. All my life of riding dicks, I had never seen such a huge one. He looked like about 12 inches. Now I understood why he kept saying, I can't handle him.

"On your knees," he demanded. Still taken aback by the size. I froze. I wasn't sure what to do. Should I back out or tackle it. I wrestled with my thoughts. I must have taken too long to fulfill the request as Orlando shook his head disapprovingly. Before he could say another word, I dropped to my knees and looked up. He smiled.

"Suck it," he said. As I started to reach my hands to wrap around it. Orlando slapped my hands away. "Mouth only," he clarified.

I complied.

I opened my mouth and extended my tongue to circle the tip of his cock. He ran his fingers through my hair then pushed my head forward, pressing his cock deep into my mouth. I tried to keep my gag reflex and my breathing steady, as he moved his hips towards me and my head towards his cock. I could only take half of it in. I could feel my eyes watering. My hands reached to his legs grabbing them for balance. I tried to keep my jaw opened as much as possible as he moved my head back and forth. But then at one point he made a huge thrust, landing almost all his shaft to the back of my throat and I suddenly gagged hard, trying not to vomit as I reflexively pulled away. I had given a few blow jobs in the past, but this was different. As a matter of fact, this was not a blow job, this was my first fuck face. I sat on the floor breathing heavily.

"Have you had enough?"

My eyes shot back up at him as I responded, "hell no." I liked the challenge.

Orlando laughed and walked past me leaving me on the floor as he removed his boxers completely then made his way to the bed. I followed him nervously. He reached for a condom then rolled it down on his dick. I found myself thinking about where he would have gotten a condom to fit that monstrosity of a cock. I laid on the bed and shivered a bit as he hovered teasingly over me. I could tell he was proud about the size of his dick, and he could tell that I was intimidated by the size of his dick. He began to slow stroke me, taking care not to put all his weight on me. He slowly pushed, and I whimpered and moaned.

"Shhhh...relax. Let me stretch this pussy baby..." I continued squealing and moaning. I felt him pushing an inch more each time. "Relax baby." He slowly grinded his way in pushing in an inch at a time.

"Fuck....it hurts." I took in a deep and slow breath. I felt like I was running a marathon.

"Have you had enough?" he asked pausing his thrust.

Every time he asked that, I feel the need to prove him wrong. I couldn't answer. He continued to stroke looking me in the eyes. I am pretty sure he could see the mix of fear and excitement in them.

"I will be easy on you tonight. I admire the effort."

He pushed in another inch. "Let big daddy make love to this sweet tight pussy. Just relax." He gave me some tongue action, and I relaxed briefly as he pushed another inch inside of me. I gasped and tears filled my eyes. He slowly stroked and pushed another inch before pulling out. He nibbled on my nipples then moved down to my navel then back up. He kissed me gently then inserted once more. He pushed a little further each time. I arched my back and moaned. "It's almost in baby, just 2 more inches to go." I closed my eyes and twisted my face in agony and grunt. He pushed another inch in. I tossed my head back. He reached up under me and pressed on my clit. I gasped and moaned again. I didn't think it was anatomically possible for me to handle all that dick, but I was determined to get every inch in. He pushed another inch in. I screamed even louder.

"It's all in now baby. Relax. Let this dick do what it got to do." He pulled out then pushed back in, stroking my walls. I could feel my pussy being torn open as it was thrusted deep inside of me. By this time, I was in tears. As he thrusted even harder and faster, I felt a fullness I had never before felt.

"Do you want me to stop?" My response was wordless, just heavy breathing as I tried to get accustomed to 12 inch cock ramming my insides. He thrusted even harder. "Do you want me to stop?" he asked again.

"No" a single word finally escaped from my mouth, as I tried not to pass out from the overwhelming sensation.

Speeding up his thrusts, he fucked me like he wanted to send me through the mattress and onto the floor. I was only able to grunt and make guttural sounds one might while going through an out of body experience. He ravaged my pussy until I heard him scream "I'm coming." He tightened up and released it all inside me. Orlando rolled off me and laughed.

"You proved me wrong."

I looked over at him and smiled. One thing I knew for sure, was that after that night, my pussy would never again be the same. I gave myself about 20 minutes to regain my composure before I drove home.

12

The drive home was very excruciating. By the time I arrived, my entire pelvic region was sore. It hurt badly to urinate, so I dreaded going to the bathroom. If I coughed or sneezed, my vagina cramped. I felt like my organs were shifted from their original positions. But as painful as the experience was, I contemplated a round 2. I had never met any man who was packing like that. I wondered what the size of his dick actually was. I think I was going to welcome this new penis length into my life and have fun with it for a short while. I prepared a warm bath, added Epsom salt and took a nice long soak with the hope that this would help to soothe my aching vagina. About an hour later, I went to bed.

The next morning I awoke to Michael standing over me.

"What the hell?" I yelled easing myself up. I really needed to get the darn locks changed so this son of bitch can stop creeping.

"Are you here with the signed papers?"

He hissed his teeth.

"Then why the hell are you here?"

"You think I am going to allow you to disrespect me and

everything I stand for? I worked hard to build every organization that even you are benefitting from. I have too much of a fragile reputation, so you need cut the bullshit."

I remained silent as I tried to figure out where this stemmed from?

He continued, "As the wife of a CEO of renowned franchises, you can't be seen with other men much less publicly flirting at business conferences. What's wrong with you?"

With that said, I finally realized what this was about. I bet it was that uneven brows witch who sat at my table. She was the same person I caught spying on me at the bar with Orlando.

"We are not together, so I can do as I please...Furthermore, I was merely socializing..."

"You better cut that crap. You are my wife and you will act accordingly."

"So let me just try to understand this situation. You are upset about me being seen socializing with others, because you believe I am embarrassing you and tarnishing your reputation, your business and every brand that you worked so hard to build? Is this correct?"

"Yes. I am glad you got the picture."

"But being seen socializing at gay clubs and fucking men in your office is in line with your brand and your reputation?"

He remained silent.

"Don't twist the scenario?"

"I am not twisting anything. You don't think people are eyeing Mr. CEO of renowned franchises when he is in public? Or is it because no one has reported anything you believe that people are oblivious to what's happening? It's only a matter of time. You just remember that what's in the dark must come to light. So you need to get your sex life together. Do you ever stop to imagine how the wife may feel knowing her husband is out somewhere with a man doing Lord knows what? Do you ever imagine that just like you, I may be a bit embarrassed?" I looked him dead in the eyes.

"How can we fix this Jos?

"Give me the divorce. Free yourself from my embarrassing social habits and continue to live your best life."

"That's not an option."

"Well allow me to live mine then."

"You are not even a promiscuous woman. What's wrong with you? Why are you trying so desperately to be that way?"

"What's wrong with me? It's more like what happened to me. I caught my husband fucking another man in our house without a condom; then again at his fucking office for a second time in less than two weeks. How does one come to terms with that?"

"I am sorry Joslyn..."

"No you are not. You would have stopped seeing him if you truly were sorry. You are only sorry that you got caught."

"But you threw me out the house and pretty much wanted nothing to do with me."

"So me throwing you out the house granted you rights to continue your sexual rendezvous?" I sighed. The truth is I was tired of the back and forthing. I didn't want to talk to him anymore, and I couldn't imagine being with him after what he did. I just wanted the divorce.

"Michael please, just leave. Please don't make this any harder for me. Furthermore, it's way too early in the morning for me to be getting this worked up. Please, I am asking you kindly, to leave?"

He didn't protest. He granted my wishes. I waited until the sun was fully out before dialing the locksmith. Then started my daily routine.

13

I gave George a call the moment I got to work because I hadn't seen him since his diagnosis and I haven't really been hearing much from him. I got through to him on the third attempt and we chatted for briefly before I resumed my day. He was in good spirits, and he reassured me that all was well.

My next client was Greg; who was back for a second session way sooner than anticipated.

"I think I am in love."

I laughed. "I guess she was very receptive towards your anal fetish?" I responded.

"NO...I haven't touched her, but he was everything."

"He?" I asked sounding slightly confused.

"Yes, I had sex with a very sexy mature hunk who seems to be loaded with money."

I remained silent. I was still taken aback by how he totally deviated from everything we discussed.

"After I left here the other day, later that night, I checked out this gay club I have always heard about. That's when I saw him. A very refined, well-groomed gentleman who seemed to be about 15 years older than I am. I immediately liked his eyes, his smile and his quiet confidence. He doesn't dominate but somehow you want to follow his lead. I accepted his drink offer and as we conversed my cock swelled in my pants. We both wanted the same thing. So we left and headed to an apartment he had nearby which was modern and lavish, but I didn't have time to enjoy it because he stripped me the moment we entered. I could tell by the way he rambled that he was very eager to relay his sexual escapades with his new gay lover.

"Spare me the details please. So you are here because you are dick whipped?"

"Sort of. I don't want to be doing this. I love my girlfriend."

"Then talk to her…The sooner you do, the better able you are to make decisions about these fantasies of yours and what you really want. In the meantime, do not indulge in any more of these encounters until you talk to her. That way the situation doesn't become too complicated. It's unfair to her for you to be running around with both sexes. I won't allow you to come back here, if it's not with an update about your relationship. Do you hear me Greg?"

"Yes, Joslyn."

"Good…I believe that would be all?"

"I believe so…Thanks Joslyn. Have a great day"

We exchanged hugs before he left.

I dialed Orlando and we agreed to meet up for lunch at one of my favourite spots.

****

He entered the restaurant, casually attired in sweat suit. Looking sexy as usual.

"Coming from the gym?" I asked as I reached up to hug him.

"Yes... I believe I work there."

"Oh," I said feeling slightly embarrassed about how little I knew about him.

"How long have you been an instructor?"

"About three years, but I am also a teacher by profession; a history teacher"

"Interesting. Most instructors I know are teachers of physical education. I don't hear this often."

"Well I am a rare breed."

"You sure are," I responded with a smirk reminiscing on how well endowed he was.

"What are we doing here" he asked bluntly.

"What do you mean?"

"I feel like you are trying to get to know me. Remember

I told you from the beginning, I want no form of attachments."

I wasn't sure how to feel about his statement. It was a little off-putting.

"I heard you and I understand but I don't think having lunch is getting attached?"

"Look, all I am saying is, if you want to fuck then say so or text it if you are afraid to. There is no need for dates, dinners or any formality. I will service you and keep it moving."

"How long have you been doing this?"

"This arrangement with you, would be the first. Normally bitches pay me to fuck them, whether in cash or kind but there is something about you. You have this look in your eyes, this burning desire to explore, so I won't pressure you. I will screw you for free."

My mind reeled. His bluntness always leaves me feeling slightly flushed. I wasn't sure what to make of the situation. But it was something to think about.

"You are a good woman, don't force it, if it's not your thing. I have to leave, but if you want to see me later, give me a call."

He then kissed me on the cheek then left.

I suddenly lost my appetite. I replayed his words. "Bitches pay me to fuck them." And just like that, that line was stuck on repeat.

Orlando s a gigolo. No wonder he was so conceited and

executed as skillfully as he did in the bedroom. I could tell that he had years of practice. I knew I was trotting a risky path but I wanted to satisfy my curiosity once more. I finished my meal then returned to work.

****

It must have been the challenge of fucking him that kept me wanting more, so I sent Orlando a text message with my address. I quickly got to the point and told him exactly what I wanted from him that night.

I was an equal amount of eager and horny. So I literally sat close to the door awaiting his arrival. As soon as he entered the front door, I was all over him. Clearly, he felt the same way, because he quickly flipped me over and ate me like he was starving. He dropped his pants, rolled on a condom and was about to penetrate me when I did the unthinkable. I told him I wanted it in the ass tonight. He grabbed me by my hair and yanked my head back then gave it to me hard, just the way I liked it. I was on my knees, back arched, head pressed deep into the pillow and he is in back of me, ass pulled apart, dick deep inside me. He reached under and slid his fingers in my wetness while he continued to pound my ass.

"Oh, shit....aaaaah....shit...oh yes baby..."

"Yeah, you like this dick, don't you?"

I moaned even louder. I clutched and unclutched his fingers with the walls of my vagina while rotating my hips. I pushed back hard and bounced on his dick. "Oh yes Orlando...bust this ass open baby" He thrust even harder. "Oh God..Yesss...." I looked over my shoulders at him pounding away and this made me even more aroused. He banged my back in for about half hour before finally nutting. He collapsed onto his back and pulled me into his arms. I lay my head on his chest as I tried to catch my breath.

"This is a nice place you have."

"Thank you..."

He kissed me lightly on my lips, pulled me even closer to his chest then drifted off to sleep.

The way I took all that dick in my ass, I feel like it would be a matter of time before shit started staining my drawers. My poor ass muscles were under pressure. I may need an ass plug to keep everything in. I laid wide awake for about one hour before waking him up. I was not about to allow him to get too comfortable at my place because he realized it was "nice". I hope his blunt ass could handle me being blunt about him leaving. I shook him even harder and this time, and soon he was wide awake.

"Damn babe, what's up?"

"You need to go!"

"What….right now?"

"Yes…."

"You can't be serious?"

"I don't need company to sleep."

It's obvious that he was surprised by my response but I was merely giving him a taste of his own medicine.

"Like you said, no formalities, just sex, no strings attached." I said smiling. It felt so good to direct his own words at him.

"Alright Joslyn." He dressed, kissed me once more then left.

14

I survived the anal encounter. Based on what went down that night, I didn't think I would have been able to carry on as normal. I thought that I would have had several bodily fluid accidents based on how he handled me, but I was fine – surprisingly. Thanks, in parts to my handy and life-saving Epsom salts soak. But the hassle was worth it though. This encounter opened my appetite, and I wanted more. I was craving everything. Anal, oral, vaginal; I yearned for all my holes to be penetrated. Though I have never participated in anything like that, I felt like today I was willing to get nasty with as many persons as possible. I called Orlando, told him my fantasies and of course he had a solution. I could tell by his willingness that "Mr. Gigolo" rarely ever backed down from a challenge.

Apparently there was a place in town that organized an orgy every week but it was via invitation only. Orlando being a key participant, hinted that he had had quite a few. We met at a bar and he insisted that I had several shots plus drinks, in order to be relaxed. He said women like me usually got cold feet when they come in very sober and he wasn't about to let me ruin the night of what he referred to as "bliss". At the bar, he introduced me to a woman by the name Saphire. She was very attractive and a flirt. She commanded my attention the minute she arrived, and we had an interesting conversation.

On our way to the secret location, Saphire kissed me intimately on the lips. We made out for a few minutes on the back seat of the car before she told me to lay down and spread my legs. I did as I was told.

Saphire leaned in, slipped her hands between my legs and began massaging my pussy. She kissed the insides of my thighs, working her way up to my breasts. She lowered her lips to my pussy once more and sucked it vigorously, so I couldn't help but to let out a moan. At this point, I felt the car stop. As she sucked the life from my vagina, I looked over at Orlando who was stroking his dick hard and fast.

"Eat her pussy…" he groaned. She continued licking and lapping. "Yes bitch, tongue fuck that pussy." The more Orlando talked trash, the more turned on she became, the faster the movement of her tongue and the more pleasure I experienced.

"You both need to eat each other at once," Orlando suggested. Saphire paused and shifted her body into the 69 position. Her pussy hovered over my face.

"Eat it babe," urged Orlando. I disobeyed the command but after a little more coaxing, I finally did as I was told. "There you go," cheered Orlando who was thoroughly enjoying the moment. "That's right babe, warm up because tonight you will be in for a treat."

He moaned and stroked his dick even harder, then Saphire began moaning, and all that moaning turned me on even more. We went at it for a few more minutes before switching positions. Saphire threw her left leg over my right leg, then we started to scissor each other. It felt so good. We moaned in unison, as we tried to make each other come.

"Yes get them pussies wet….oh fuck… I am gonna nut. Fuck!" Next thing I knew, Saphire quickly hopped off me then Orlando positioned himself on his knees in the front seat and he continued to stroke vigorously. I could tell that this was something they had both done before. I sat up and watched as she positioned herself and braced for the routine. She opened her mouth wide and I watched as Orlando squirts semen down her throat and she guzzles it all down. She was hungry for it. The bitch didn't want to share any of it, and that was totally fine by me. When she was finished, she leaned over and grabbed me by the back of my head then shoved her tongue down my mouth. We were swapping spit and come back & forth. Orlando grinned.

"I think she is ready for tonight" Orlando said looking at Saphire then back at me. I smiled.

****

As I walked gingerly behind Saphire and Orlando down a very dark hallway, I began feeling a little nervous. I am not sure how I had gotten to this point in my life, but I was not about to stop now. A gap was being filled, and I was liking it. I couldn't tell what gap it was, but despite my nervousness, I didn't care. We entered a room that was very dimly lit. Some persons were walking around naked, some were semi clothed, some wore mask, and it seemed to be one big room with subdivisions.

"I think you may be interested in what's behind door number 2. Don't be shy, just have fun," Orlando said kissing me on the lips then disappearing with Saphire. I slowly approached door # 2, and I felt my stomach flutter. For a moment, I thought I heard a familiar voice. I entered and gazed at a very handsome, topless, chocolate skinned man. He looked like a model. He introduced his self as Miguel. He was followed by a sexy light skin dude named Mario who had caramel eyes. The last man was slow to recede from the shadows, and when I set my gaze on him, I felt my entire body go still in absolute shock.

I knew that I had heard a familiar voice and sure enough my ears did not deceive me. When I looked into the alluring, intoxicating blue eyes of my husband's best friend, I found my womb aching in absolute desire. This was me finally getting even with him.

"You are absolutely gorgeous," Kevin said, gently

skimming my cheeks with his fingers. "I am Kevin," he said playing his role. My lips parted for a few fleeting moments before I found my voice again. "Thank you Kevin."

He ran his hands along my navel down to my pelvic region, and I closed my eyes and purr against his tender touch. He then framed my face with his large hands, forcing me to gaze into his beautiful eyes. He planted a kiss on my lips, which grew deeper until our tongues entangled. Kevin kisses my neck.

"I can't wait to fuck this wet pussy." He whispered.

Hearing his sexy decadent voice in my ear sent a shudder of primal lust pulsating through me. I felt a pair of hands reaching from behind to caress my breasts. He unzipped my dress, and exposed my body. I felt the coalescing, collective lust of all three men directly focused on me. I felt a tingle in my stomach. This was surreal and completely out of my comfort zone; I couldn't believe I was actually about to participate in this scene. Strangely, I was pleased, because my fantasy was being fulfilled. Kevin went behind me then Mario wrapped his lips around my left nipple then Miguel wrapped his lips around my right nipple. Suddenly, a strong wave of arousal flooded my womb and a gasp escaped me. Kevin glided his fingers along my slit and teased me. Mario and Miguel started sucking my nipples harder, then someone inserted a finger at the same time. Kevin grinded his hips against me, making me whimper when I felt his straining erection rub against my ass.

"I want to fuck your throat and your ass."

I was the most excited about him, for obvious reasons. My eyes rolled back as a ragged moan escaped me. He grinded his cock against my ass even more, and as I focused on the sexy wet sounds of Mario and Miguel sucking the soul out of my breasts and pussy, I was drowning in absolute euphoria.

Kevin and Miguel unbuckled their pants. I dropped to my knees and moaned fervently as I felt a gush of moisture between my legs. I spat on both my palms before bringing the two long, beautiful, thick cocks to my mouth. I wrapped my hands around their veiny shafts and stroked them sensually, making sure to spread my warm, slick saliva all over their cocks. I flicked my tongue against the hot slit of Miguel's penis then I wrapped my lips around the fat velvety cockhead. Miguel groaned and pumped his hips against my hot mouth.

"Suck this dick baby...Just like that...Yess...Ahhhh.."

The unified sounds coming from the three of them were music to my ears, because I loved hearing men's guttural groans of pleasure.

The other men were way too turned on to wait their turn. They rolled on a condom then the next thing I noticed, was Mario laying on the floor; he positioned me on top of him and penetrated my pussy. Miguel positioned himself in such a way that I was able to continue sucking his cock while leaning forward allowing Kevin to penetrate my ass.

"Take this dick bitch...Feel this long cock in your wet little pussy." I could see that Mario was just as good a trash talker like Orlando but this seemed to entice Kevin because he ravaged my ass even more. I felt my pussy throb, and I let out a scream. Mario gripped my neck tightly forcing me to pull back from Miguel's cock.

"Cum on this cock bitch."

The two men continued to thrust into me meanwhile raw, potent, ecstasy paralyzed my body. My cum gushed out of me making my body violently tremble in absolute unfiltered pleasure. They all groaned in approval and satisfaction and continued to thrust.

"Spill your hot thick cum inside my pussy and ass. Fuck my slutty hole," I said and all three men went wild. I continued the trash talk and this pushed Mario over the edge. He gasped and released his cum inside me. His orgasm triggered Miguel's orgasm which in turn triggered Kevin's. I crumpled over on Mario and remained that way for a few minutes.

I recomposed myself and geared up for round 2. After all, I didn't get a chance to properly service Miguel. Unfortunately, this was not going to happen because Orlando and Saphire entered the room.

"Excuse me gentlemen, but I need this lady," Orlando said sternly. They were all very obedient, and they left the room. Saphire hopped on the couch and no sooner did I spread her legs and buried my face into her pussy greedily. Her moans triggered Orlando, and he started to moan; I could tell that they were both heated. I moved my face, allowing Orlando to slide inside of her. He hovered over her then inserted his dick, as she wrapped her legs around his waist. She moaned; I grabbed and squeezed her breasts then nibbled on her nipples. As he deep stroked Saphire, I went behind him and played with his ass. I circled my fingers around his hole, and I felt him tightened. I then lightly brushed my tongue against his ass hole, then he began screaming like a bitch. The high pitch of his yelp frightened me at one point. That shit turned him on so much. The more I licked his asshole, the harder he pounded and stretched Saphire's hole. I bit him on his ass cheeks then kissed him along his spine. I then nibbled on his earlobe for a few seconds after which he craned his head towards me, and I slipped my tongue in his mouth. We slobbed each other down as he simultaneously pounded Saphire"s pussy. She was screaming and moaning and digging her fingers into his back. Orlando started to talk bedroom trash until they both exploded.

Their combined raw, simmering ecstasy was too much for me... I came one final time...

****

We were all so drained after the night's "sexcapade" that a usual 40 minutes' drive, took us almost two hours. When I finally made it home, I fell asleep twice while attempting to shower. I was definitely taking the day or possibly the rest of the week off. My body needed a full recovery. I had an awesome night though, and I would definitely do that again. The highlight for me was that I fucked Mikey's best friend, and it felt so good. I should pick up the phone and tell him now; I am sure that would grant me a divorce. I laughed hysterically. I flung myself onto the bed and called it a night.

15

That orgy seemed to have released a type of sex demon in me. I took the time off from work to break some more rules and carry on in manners that I had never before imagined. I agreed to another blissful encounter with the deacon; only this time it was at his house. The ladies in my office often times teased about Christians being one of the freakiest set of people, but after my first encounter with Mr. Wesley, I was beginning to think there was some truth to the claims. Some are just supposedly discrete with it since they are supposed to live in accordance with the Word. But Mr. Wesley was one of a kind. He was not the ordinary freak; he was a top notch freak.

He welcomed me with a glass of baileys rum cream and wasted no time. Before I halved my glass, he nestled his head between my legs and did what he did best. There was something about the way he did it. He was a cunnilingus connoisseur. I was about to orgasm but then the next few words he uttered totally destroyed the moment.

"Piss in my mouth. Let me feel your strong, steamy flow of hot golden urine on my tongue. Then take my dick and fuck it like you own it."

The look on my face showed my utter displeasure. I scratched my head as I tried to process his request.

"I have been dying to have a woman like you with a wet pussy to hose me down with piss. To be perfectly honest, you know what would turn me on even more?"

Honestly I was afraid to find that out. I hesitated before responding. "What would that be?"

"If you could squat over me and shit on my stomach while I am playing in your pussy," he nodded licking his lips. "Oh God, the thought of it is turning me on so much."

"Jesus is going to tear your ass up on judgement day, I responded."

"I will pray about it. He will forgive me and I will be good as new to enter the pearly gates."

I wondered how many screws this nigga lost, because there was no way he could actually be comfortable with what he just said.

"Why do you look so startled baby?"

"Because you are one nasty son of a bitch who is going straight to hell."

"I thought you said you were open minded and liked it nasty?"

"I am open to a lot of things but smelling piss and shit while I am trying to fuck is not one of them."

I should have bounced on his nasty ass but I ended up

fucking him anyway. I told him I would grant his request at the end, just in case I ended up freaking myself out, at least I would have gotten the fuck I came for.

He rambo fucked me and as I promised, I squatted over him and pissed all over his nasty ass, hitting him in the face and mouth. He opened up and slurped the piss like a hot cup of chocolate.

I ran to the bathroom and threw up in the toilet bowl. Then again, maybe I should have let it out on spot, in his presence. If faeces turned him on then I don't see why vomit wouldn't. I wasted no time at his place. I rinsed my mouth, gargled with some mouthwash, and I was out.

You best believe he wanted to kiss me. I eased him off. Not after I found out that, that mouth of his has possibly eaten loads of shit. I felt my stomach churn at the thought.

"It's like that baby?" He seemed confused that I was leaving.

"Enjoy the rest of the evening," I said.

I bolted out the house and backed out of that driveway at lightning speed. It's safe to say I was done with Mr. Wesley. May the Lord be with him.

16

A week later, I decided to end my vacation in "sex land" and returned to normalcy. As luck would have it, my day began with drama. I was greeted by a large envelope on my desk from a law firm. I opened it and the letter read:

Dear Mrs Sharpalova,

We represent a young woman employee of CBN who has been the victim of constant and relentless sexual harassment by you. We are not naming the employee to prevent possible intimidation and embarrassment of the employee. The harassment has included telephone calls to the woman's residence, innuendo, an attempt at cunnilingus…..

Baffled by the first few sentences I read, I skipped to the end of the letter and resumed reading.

We are prepared to commence litigation, however, we believe that any such litigation would be extremely damaging to both companies' reputation as well as the reputation of the individuals involved. Therefore, we suggest that we meet at the earliest possible time in order to attempt to resolve this matter.

However, if we do not hear from you within 5 business days from receipt of this letter, we will have no choice but to start a lawsuit, in order to protect our client's right. We trust you understand our position...

I stopped reading. I was beyond confused. Before I had even managed to gather my thoughts, Greg busted through the door laughing hysterically. He plopped himself down on the couch and laughed even more. Honestly, I was slightly put off by what I had just read and by his out-of-place laughter, but I allowed him to laugh, while I tried to recompose myself. I packed away the letter then gathered my pen and notebook to begin my session. I stared at him until our eyes met, indicating that I was ready to begin if he was.

"I have HIV...matter of factly, I don't have HIV...I have full blown AIDS." He laughed uncontrollably once more. A few minutes later, the laughter turned to sobs.

I approached him with the intention to say something soothing but I was lost for words. Then on second thought, I wasn't sure words could comfort him at this moment, so I opted to hug him.

"Don't touch me...Didn't you hear me say I have AIDS. I will infect you." He resisted but I managed to overpower him, holding him closely. He buried his head into my bosom and sobbed even harder. I fought back the tears. I held him and rocked him... The office phone rang, but I didn't want to disturb the moment since I was finally getting him to calm down, so I ignored it. After a minute or so, it rang again and again I ignored it.

Then I heard what seemed like an argument on the other side of the door. That's when I decided to pull myself away from Greg. I stood up just in time to see Michael storming through the door infuriated.

"I am done with this. This is what you wanted right?" he said waving an envelope in the air. "Well there it is, the divorce is final. You know what. I don't even want anything from you. Keep it all. God knows how many men you have brought in that house anyway. You can have it all. We are done Joslyn. Have a nice life." He threw the envelope on the desk then stormed out.

"Mrs Sharpalova, I am so sorry. I tried to call you. I tried to stop him. I really tried. I am so sorry." She looked like she was on the brink of tears, and I didn't think I was emotionally stable to handle any more tears or any more drama for the rest of the day, so I quickly interrupted her before she broke down.

"Tiffany, its fine. Don't worry about it."

"I am sorry," she said once more before leaving.

I held my head for a few seconds. "Can my day get any worst?" I thought. Of course my train of thoughts were short-lived by Greg's hysterical laugh again.

"I must apologize for the misconduct you just witnessed. This has never happened before, and I assure you it won't happen again. I will reschedule another session, free of cost, provided that it's ok with you".

"That's your husband. Well ex-husband?"

"Yes, and I am really sorry about his behavior. Can we please set a date to re-do this session?" He laughed once more. "The hot hunk, is your husband." He laughed uncontrollably. I was beginning to feel irritated.

"Greg, I know it's hard for you to focus right now, but I will have to end this session as I have a few things I would like to sort immediately. So can we please agree on a date?"

"I slept with your husband!"

"What?"

"The hunk I talked about..."

I stood there confused.

"The sexy mature man I met at the gay club with the nice eyes, gorgeous smile and confidence that was everything?"

I remained silent.

"You know the one with the mind blowing sex who had me dick whipped? The one I could talk about all day in our sessions if you don't stop me; that.... was your husband."

He laughed hysterically again before continuing, "Well isn't life a bitch!"

My body became numb, and now all I could see was Greg sitting there laughing but there were no sounds. I watched his mouth move, but I was unable to hear anything. All his movements were now in slow motion. I felt the room getting smaller. Then reality set in, Greg has AIDS and he slept with my husband. Next thing I knew my legs buckled and my body plummetted towards the floor.

17

I woke up to the stark smell of disinfectants, invading my nostrils. The room was silent apart from my heavy breathing and that beeping sound you often hear in hospitals. I felt powerless and heavy. It was so hard to move my hands and my body. I slowly opened my eyes, squinting in an attempt to sharpen the blurred images before me. I glanced around and took in the deserted peach and white colour schemed hospital bedroom. How long have I been here? I closed my eyes, trying to remember what exactly had happened. Then it all hit me with a bang. The memory of it all started to occupy my thoughts. Just then, I noticed Tiffany sitting at the other end of the room.

"Hi Mrs Sharpolova...How are you feeling?"

"I feel very weak."

"Hopefully you will feel better after resting. You scared us all today. I didn't know who else to call so I called your husband," she looked down at the floor after she said this.

"Thank you Tiffany. You have been very helpful today. Thank you for being there."

A few seconds later, the devil entered the room in his usual fine style.

"I am not going to do this with you. You asked for a divorce and I gave it to you. I am no longer the person you should call or ask for help whenever you have your meltdowns. I am done Joslyn. This is the last time I will show up for you. I am sure you have other men you can call."

Wow, I thought. When did he become so disrespectful? The Mikey I knew would never say certain things publicly, especially in the presence of our employees but now, he didn't seem to care at all. Why does he seem to resent me so much? The truth is it was fair to say that I was the victim. I know we are getting divorced but is it really possible for a person's feelings towards someone they have loved for years, to change that quickly? As much as I slept around, I still missed him. But I guess he was right. He should no longer be my emergency contact.

"I am sorry to have disturbed your day. It won't happen again," was all I managed to say. I really didn't want to waste the little energy I had left quarreling with Mikey.

The doctor entered and did his routine checks before offering to provide an update. I asked Michael and Tiffany to leave the room.

"No, I want to make sure you are ok" he protested.

"You could have fooled me. After that grand entrance? As you rightfully said, this is no longer your duty." I responded. "You made it abundantly clear, so please leave!" He turned to look at me for a mere second, nodded his head as if to agree then left without a word.

As soon as he did, the doctor proceeded.

"Your blood pressure is elevated but other than that, you and the baby seem to be well."

"What?"

"Everything is ok…You just need to take it easy a bit," repeated the doctor.

"You said the baby and I are well?"

"That's right!"

"I am pregnant?"

The doctor looked at me astonished.

"You were not aware of this?"

"I didn't think I could get pregnant. My husb…" I paused then restructured my sentence. "I tried for months to conceive. I have exhausted fertility regimens and still nothing happened."

"Oh wow…Well with that, said I will do a thorough examination of you and the baby and get back to you. In the meantime, I would prefer to keep you here tonight? Will that be ok?"

"Yes that will be fine. OMG doc, I am pregnant," I screamed.

"I am actually having a baby!"

The doctor laughed.

Then it hit me… "OMG doc, what if I have HIV…Will I

give it to my baby? Oh my God...No..No..No.." Reality started to set in.

"Hold on, calm down please. I need to understand what's happening with you. Are you HIV positive?"

"I don't know. I have been exposed, so there is a possibility. I have also been drinking. I hope I didn't cause any harm to my child. Oh god!"

"Let's get you tested first, then we can proceed from there. I need you to relax though and get some rest. Can you promise me that?"

"Yes but doc, what happens if my results come back positive?"

"Then we start you on treatment straight away and you have to take it every day for the rest of your life. If you take your treatment correctly, it will lower the amount of the virus in your body so much that it is said to be undetectable or what we refer to as an undetectable viral load. This means that you can plan to have a normal, vaginal delivery because the risk of passing HIV to your baby during childbirth would be extremely small. If you don't have an undetectable viral load, you may be offered a caesarean section, as this carries a smaller risk of passing HIV to your baby than a vaginal delivery. Your baby would also be given treatment for four to six weeks after birth to help prevent an HIV infection developing. We will test the baby at birth and again 4-6 weeks later. If the results are negative, we will test again at 18 months"

"What about breastfeeding?" I know I was getting ahead of myself, but I truly couldn't help it. This was a lot to take in all at once, and the doctor could tell.

"How about you let us get the process started then based on your results, I will brief you on everything accordingly. I don't want to overwhelm you with information right now."

"Ok..Sounds like a plan."

When he left, Tiffany came back into the room. I gave her instructions to contact and inform the clients I had scheduled for the rest of the week about my absence from the office. I remembered my pending lawsuit but then that was too much of a personal matter to get Tiffany involved. I would just have to find a way to sort that on my own. Tiffany and I wrapped up the weekly to do list, and I thanked her again for being so supportive. She then left to go home.

I closed my eyes and basked in the thoughts of finally becoming a mother. I was so excited, but I was also worried about the health of my baby. I prayed that I wouldn't transfer the virus to my baby, in the event my results tested positive. I kept the happy thoughts active until I drifted to sleep.

18

"Good Morning gorgeous," the doctor entered the room beaming as if he had just won the lottery. I could tell that he was one of those perky morning persons. The nurses followed shortly after with breakfast. I can't believe I slept through the entire night.

"I have good news," the doctor said, still beaming from ear to ear. I am not sure why, but his happiness was irritating me. "You are a healthy mother; the only issue is that your blood pressure is still elevated. I remained silent. "That means you are HIV negative," he continued, I guess trying to get a more favorable response from me. I smiled.

"Well I am relieved to hear that," I finally said.

"I will ask that you repeat the test in a few months, for a more accurate prognosis". "If you want, we could arrange for an ultrasound to be done today."

"Yes, I would love that." Though it didn't show, I was elated.

"I will allow you to eat and snap out of your morning funk, before I send someone in."

"I am sorry," I said realizing that my somber disposition was evident.

"There is nothing to be sorry about; I understand."

After they all left the room. I dialed Tiffany just to go over the list of things that needed to be accomplished like the true workaholic I am. She told me that of all my clients, George and Gregg were the most concerned about my well-being. I took George's number and decided that I would give him a call as soon as I got home. We chatted for a few minutes more before proceeding with our day. I had my breakfast, but the whole time I was wondering how to move forward with this new revelation.

Should I tell Mikey that I was pregnant? But then again, I was not sure I wanted a man who was confused by his sexuality to be around my child. On the other hand, I never imagined raising a child on my own.

"Oh Lord why now? I have been trying for so long, and this is the time you have chosen to make it happen. My life is such a mess right now?" I thought. But then for a brief moment I wondered if the child was even for my husband? I drank the last of my eight ounce glass of water that was given to me in preparation for the ultrasound. I reminisced on my sexual escapades, and to my recollection, a condom was always in place. I didn't recall ever having any mishaps. I thought it through thoroughly about three more times before convincing myself that the child was in fact for Mikey.

One hour later, the technician came in with the machine to get started. I felt excited. This was actually happening. My first ultrasound. She placed a cold gel on my abdomen and moved the wand-like device all over the area. Several moments later, there it was. I saw my little bake bean with a strong heartbeat. Suddenly, I was filled with mixed emotions. When they told me, I was about 3 months pregnant. I still couldn't believe this was happening. It was all good news. She reassured me that all was well but that the doctor still needed to review the findings for confirmation.

After they left, I wasn't sure what to do with the rest of the day. I was so accustomed to working all the time that it was very hard for me to laze in the hospital despite knowing and completely understanding that that I was in dire need of rest.

Just as I was in between thoughts and trying to figure out my next move, a message came in from Orlando. "Hey sexy, when are you coming to wet this dick?" This was followed by another text, only this time it was from Mr. Wesley. I have not heard from him in quite a while.

"I see you have forgotten about me."

"Not at all, just been busy. How are you?" I was trying to sound normal.

"Missing you? Can we meet up for lunch or dinner?"

"I don't think so. I am not feeling too well."

Even if I was feeling ok, I would have still found

another excuse. Truth be told, I was never really into him. Things got a bit awkward after the last "messy" sexual encounter. As much as I enjoyed discovering my wild side, I was not ready for that level of freakiness. Truthfully, that was outside of my realm of sexual desires and I was experiencing immense guilt for having gotten intimately involved with him being my client. I was bothered that he was so comfortable with it. While I didn't go to church, I was fearful that God was somehow punishing me, and I felt this even more now that I was pregnant. Having waited all this time, I didn't want anything happening to this child. Of all the encounters I had had, the only person I could see myself with, if I were to mess with anyone, would be Orlando.

However, I allowed his message to linger while I tuned in to the television until I eventually fell asleep.

19

Tiffany stormed through the room door frantically... "This doesn't look good Joslyn. This doesn't look good." I could barely open my eyes, but I could hear her pacing the room.

"What could possibly have you so worked up at this time of the day?" I asked as I eased myself up on the bed and allowed the light to finally penetrate my eyes. She threw the newspaper in my lap.

The headline read: *Extramarital affairs…. CEO of a renowned franchise flirts with young brunette while wife is hospitalized.* I read through the article and scoffed. Not even 48 hours had passed and he was already flirting with someone else. I wondered how long that affair had been going on. I wondered if she had anything to do with him finally signing the papers. Well at least he was caught flirting with a woman. The tabloids would have had a field day had it been anything else.

"She is gorgeous; he sure knew how to pick them", I thought as I continued to stare at the paper.

"So…." Poor Tiffany. She had no clue what was going on and was evidently more bothered than I cared to be.

"So what?" I was blasé.

"Why are you so calm? Why aren't you on the phone cussing his ass out for what he did? That is just plain disrespectful"

"Don't worry about it." I said trying to calm her down.

"You could have died. He couldn't wait to leave here the other day... why...to go get his freak on with some young brunette?"

"Tiff...this is not your battle to fight. Stop taking it so personal. Furthermore, the last thing I need is for something else to stress me."

"I want to be like you when I grow up". I could tell that she was confused and relieved at the same time.

We both laughed.

"One thing I have learnt is that you could be drop dead gorgeous, excellent in bed, cook like chef Bourdain, if a man decides to cheat, nothing you do will stop him".

"So are you saying it's ok for him to cheat?"

"Definitely not...but getting upset right now, while hospitalized won't help my current state either. Besides, Mr. Sharpolova no longer has any obligations to me. He is a free man." This time I was more nonchalant.

She looked at me puzzled.

"We are divorced."

"What...As in..." She paused.

"Yes. As in completed paperwork and all. Officially divorced." I looked away as I tried to fight the tears. Not solely because of the divorce but just the whole outcome. How badly I wanted a family and now all of that was broken.

"I am sorry…" Tiffany was close to tears and clueless as to what else to say to me.

"Just one of those things…life goes on". I paused for a little bit and allowed her to gather her composure from the shock of the information she had just received. "Anyway, enough of the pity party. How was work? Did you complete all on the list?"

"Yes I did…" She was still trying to process the information.

"Great, so if all goes well I should be back to regular schedule on Monday."

"Are you rested?"

"I have a business to run. If I stay any longer in here, I am bound to lose my mind. Thanks for everything Tiff," I said with arms stretched to hug her.

"Is there anything else I can get you?"

"I think you have covered it all." Then I remembered that I needed to address my sexual harassment lawsuit.

"Set up a meeting with my lawyer for Monday please," then that will be all".

The doctor and nurses came in to do their routine checks; my vitals had improved, so I was being discharged. I sent a text to Orlando telling him to meet me at my place.

I pretty much lazed and chatted with Tiffany until it was time to leave the hospital.

20

Since finding out about my pregnancy, I was catapulted into a state of confusion that I had never before experienced. On the one hand, I was excited about the prospects of having a baby, especially having tried everything in the past to become pregnant. On the other hand, I was unsure about how I would make this work, especially now that the divorce had become finalized, which meant becoming a single parent. This was not something I anticipated nor would even fathom be my reality. I was also in a state of confusion because of my sexual attraction to Orlando and the type of wild sex we were having.

But I knew that this had to stop. I wanted it to stop. As much as I had a connection with Orlando, I didn't see our interaction moving outside of what it was – a fucking one!

Apart from those present at the hospital the day I found out, doctors included, no one else knew of the pregnancy.

As confused as I was, I was also a little turned on just thinking about Orlando's package. But the thought of creating a more stable situation for this unborn child was more pronounced than anything else. I needed to make this right.

My thoughts were soon interrupted by the doorbell. It was Orlando. I could tell he was excited to see me. Was he rubbing his dick on his way here? He was already aroused by the time he entered the front door.

Everything that happened between me opening the door and me being completely naked was a blur. The next thing I knew I was on top of him and doing exactly what I wanted to no longer do.

Beads of sweat shot out from every pore of my body. With eyes closed, I rode his dick like a champion. While in the midst of my performance, I had flashbacks of Michael having the time of his life with Eli in his office. The more my thoughts traveled, the faster I rode to combat the heartbreak I felt. Orlando guided my butt up and down, repeatedly ramming his enormous twelve inch pole through a maze of juicy flesh. He rubbed my ultra-sensitive clitoris back and forth as if trying to speed up the race. This turned me on so much that I could feel my insides spilling out juices in joyful response.

"Oh fuck!!!!! Yes...Yes.. Don't stop baby. Don't stop. Right there..Yes..O shit!!!" I was about to come.

Orlando was about to have his orgasm from watching my performance. He loved when a woman was on top and about to orgasm. I screamed, released my juices then collapsed on his chest. I held him like my life depended on it.

"Damn girl, you miss big daddy didn't you?"

I didn't respond. "Don't wait so long to see me next time."

We didn't usually cuddle, but I felt like I needed to be pampered today, and he didn't question it.

"You had a long week?"

"Kind of... "

"I saw the paper. I am sorry it happened like that?"

"What?" I asked

"With your husband caught cheating or flirting, whatever it was."

I forgot about that. I was more concerned about the life growing inside of me than I was anything else and was preoccupied with the thoughts of becoming a mother. I was trying to get used to the idea. I knew that soon everything about my life would have changed.

I was suddenly aware that I couldn't continue to live the life I was living. I needed to be careful about who I was with. I needed to be settled and soon. I was surprised that he hadn't mentioned anything to me about my body but then again, I didn't notice any change with my body either, so why would he?

"We are divorced now, so its whatever," I finally answered.

"So what will happen to the house?" he asked

I was surprised by his question. "You really like it here don't you?" I said smacking him on the arm.

"It's aiight."

"Is that why you are so concerned about whether I will keep it because it's an ok house?"

"You know you have a really nice place, so stop tripping."

I laughed. "It doesn't hurt to say it."

"Yeah. Well how do you feel now, knowing he is officially out of your life?"

"He has been gone for a little over a month before all this drama. So it's not that big of a deal!" I said, lying blatantly.

"Well if you ever need anything, I will be glad to help"

I sprung to my feet when he said this.

I could see right through Orlando's charade. He was fascinated by my house; in fact, more fascinated than he had been about anything else concerning me.

I paused for a moment and looked over at him. In that instance, I started to wonder. All I really knew about him was how big his dick was and how he liked to be fucked. I stared at him, and I could tell he was uncomfortable. He wasn't sure what I was thinking.

"Why the sudden interest in helping me Orlando?"

"All I am saying is, with your husband gone, you may need help with little things. I am here if that ever happens. No need to get ahead of ourselves now."

"Ok Mr. Orlando. Whatever you say." I became resolved. Now that I was pregnant, I really didn't want to continue on this sex path, but it was safe to say that I enjoyed him in a way that I hadn't anyone else.

"Come here, straddle up over my face," he demanded.

Unlike other times, I didn't immediately respond. I stood there looking at him. I knew this would be the last time I would be with him. I had two choices, I could either tell him or I could give him a goodbye fuck. I chose the latter. .

"Lower that pussy onto my mouth.

I did as I was told.

As he tongue- drilled me, I went nuts. He shifted me enough to be able to place his tongue in my ass while finger-popping my pussy. I wined on his tongue and moaned loudly. He sat up and made his way slowly off the bed, never letting up on my hole. He stood and held me upside down, still eating my pussy. The perks of fucking a real gym dud. They can lift and toss you all over the place. I was about to orgasm again, this time screaming at the top of my lungs. I involuntarily tightened my legs around his neck, as my body shook and released all my juices. He released me onto the bed then slumped over beside me. The rest of the evening was a blur.

The night ended soon after, and so did our interaction. That was the last time I spoke to Orlando.

21

"Jesus Christ Joslyn, sexual harassment. What the hell? We don't want another story hitting the tabloids. You and Michael need to start handling your business privately, this doesn't look good." He said storming through the door.

"Good Afternoon Mr. Green, it's nice to see you too. I don't know if I should be hurt by the fact that you barged in here automatically assuming that I am guilty."

"Well I mean, your relationship is messy at the moment so anything is possible. I am not sure what to think" he responded. "So did you do it?" he asked.

"Absolutely not," I responded.

"Then why would someone want to start such drama with you?"

"I don't know. That's what we are going to try and figure out."

"Tell me what exactly happened?"

"I was having my usual sessions. This woman came in dressed sexily. I admit, she was eye candy. Her breasts were spilling out her top. It was hard not to notice them. Anyways, I remained professional and fulfilled my duties; listening to her issues but then the unexpected happened."

Mr. Green shifted in his chair with brows raised.

"She relived a sexual encounter she had."

"What do you mean by relived a sexual encounter?"

"Nipples....started telling her friend about the guy she slept with."

"Nipples?" the lawyer asked.

"Yes the one suing me. That's what I nicknamed her because of how she arrived at the office."

"Ok continue."

"So she was telling her friend about the size of his penis and how great the sex was. The friend became turned on. Then next thing I knew, they both started kissing. Then Nipples hand traveled up her friends skirt and they were fondling and moaning and...."

"Oh shit!!!!" he interrupted.

"Exactly...And I am sitting there turned on as hell."

"Did you try to stop them?"

"Yes, twice and they ignored me, so I sat quietly and watched the ordeal. I am admitting to being turned on by the women, but I never touched them. They touched me, I should be filing a lawsuit."

"They touched you?"

"Yes. They stopped their session abruptly and next thing I knew they were focused on me. Her friend grabbed my breast and I didn't respond professionally, initially, I let my hormones get the better of me and as such she massaged them for a few more seconds but then when Nipples made a sudden grab for my vagina that's when I snapped out of it and pushed her off.

"At no point did you touch any of them? Be it for a second?"

"No...I didn't touch any of them."

"No kiss, no massage, nothing to have encouraged any of it?"

"Nothing whatsoever."

"And you wouldn't happen to have any surveillance in the office?"

"No, no surveillance."

For a brief moment, I thought about it and I am glad I didn't because the discovery of some footage would have definitely painted a negative picture on my business.

"Why would they come after you?"

We sat in silence.

"You don't think the article could have contributed to this? Maybe, they recognized who your husband was and figured they could maybe make some quick cash off you?"

I mulled it over for a second. Although it sounded plausible, I was not so sure about his proposal.

"It's not farfetched. Trust me on that. You would be amazed by the extent people go to get money," he remarked.

'So what's our next move?"

"Let's hear what they are demanding, but I think more than likely this will be settled via mediation. I wouldn't worry too much about it. If what you say is true then they don't have a case. But should you have additional information to share, please give me a call as soon as possible. I need to know everything if I am going to represent you well."

"I told you everything. That's the truth."

"Ok. Well, we will be in touch."

As he stood and gathered his things to leave, he said "And Joslyn, please stay out the media. I am not used to you being in this light."

I smiled.

"Thanks Mr. Green. I will work on it."

We exchanged kisses on the cheek before he left.

22

Why is this happening to me? I lived a very simple life and, I was happy with it. All I ever wanted was a child but now the timing was all wrong. God why have you done this to me? Why now? Why me? Everything seemed to be going wrong. Is this some form of punishment? I cried and cursed the Supreme Being in between sobs. However, my train of thought was short lived by a phone call from George. I have been meaning to call him but he first me to it.

"How have you been George?"

"I have seen better days, but I am giving thanks."

"Which is right!"

"How are you doing though?"

"I am good, thanks for asking."

"Are you really? I cannot imagine how you must have felt being hospitalized while your husband gallivants with another woman. These men I tell yah!!!"

I remained silent. I wondered if he thought because we were able to establish a good rapport during our sessions, means he is privy to my personal life.

"The media has a way of embellishing things, but I am

indeed well. Thanks for your concern George."

"And even if it was so, you would not have aired your business anyway."

Exactly, so why ask? I thought.

"You are a nice woman, and you don't deserve that but I want to just say a short prayer for you, if you don't mind?"

"Sure. Prayer can never be too much," I responded.

"Lord Mrs Sharpalova's marriage is in grave trouble. Touch her and her husband, bring them as close as they were in the beginning. Give them both the strength to love and care for each other. Heal the division between them and make them one again. In your precious name."

"Amen" we said in unison.

Beautiful prayer but unfortunately it was too late for that, I thought.

"Thanks George. Please take good care of yourself. You should come see me next week?"

"That would be nice. I will let you know closer to the time when to expect me."

"No problem. Have a great day George."

****

I took a long deep breath, before exhaling. With hands above my head and on the back of the chair, I tried to put things into perspective. I let my mind float as I reassessed my life once more. If I am to be honest with myself, I felt somewhat lost and deflated ever since the divorce was finalized. Now a baby on board, I wasn't sure I even wanted to keep it, not because I didn't want a child but because I never imagined having to do this on my own. I questioned my career and my daily routine, trying to figure out, what needed to be altered to make me and my baby as comfortable and happy as possible. I took another deep breath and reminisced about my intense sexual encounters. I had already taken the steps to change that aspect of my life, and I was pleased with myself.

As clear as I was about giving up Orlando, I wasn't as clear about Sapphire. There was something different about her. She was very refreshing and knew how to work my body. Our chemistry was amazing and not like anything else I had experienced. She was gentle, and I liked her. I wasn't sure what I would do in relation to her, and I wasn't as resolved to give her up the way I was to give up Orlando.

As if she sensed that I was thinking about her, Saphire strolled through the door dripping in sexiness. I was so surprised to see her.

"What are you doing here?" I said as I stood to hug her. She slipped her arms around my waist, pulling me to her and placing her lips as close as she could to mine without actually touching them.

Looking into my eyes, she whispered "I can't stop thinking about you since the other night. I want you all for myself."

I stepped away from her and closed the office door. "Bring that sexy ass over here" I found myself smiling girlishly.

Gripping my waist, she pulled me into her, teasing my lips with her tongue, tracing them ever so softly around the corners of my mouth. I stood there and allowed her to have her way with my body. I loved her gentle touches. She planted kisses along my shoulders, neck then returned to my lips. She kissed my whole body intensely, slowly working her way down my thighs until her face ended up between my legs. I placed one leg on my desk and instinctively pressed her head more firmly into my vagina. I closed my eyes and enjoyed every moment she slid her tongue in and out of me, moaning softly in between. My eyes rolled back in my head and memories of the three of us making love swirled through my mind resulting in my juices flowing more on her lips. But then all this niceness was suddenly interrupted by a persistent loud bang on the door. This frightened us both. I fixed my underwear and signaled for her to go clean up in the bathroom. I opened the door.

"Oh my god, you again?"

He stormed past me.

"You sure love to make an entrance don't you?"

"After everything I have done for you, this is how you repay me?" he said holding his head.

"Excuse me?"

"My wife has turned into a whore."

So shocked by the outburst and the uncertainty as to where the conversation lead, I called out to Saphire and asked her to leave.

"Are you sure, you want me to leave? Will you be ok?" she sounded terribly concerned.

Mikey's temper had gotten to her.

"I will be fine. I will call you later." I reassured her. She hugged me before leaving.

"What is this...Is this how friendly you are with your clients, you little bitch." Next thing I knew he sprung from the couch and shoved Saphire to the floor. She screamed as she fell.

"What the fuck is wrong with you?" I said slapping him in the face.

"Why are you even here?" I shouted angrily. I watched Saphire picked herself up with a slight limp as she exited the office. "I am calling the police," she said.

"No you won't," he made a second attempt to grab her.

'Mikey...stop it." I pushed him this time, he shoved me back then a fight ensued. I could hear a mixture of screams and cries coming from Saphire and my assistants.

"Have you fucking lost your mind….Why are you here?" By this time he had me in a chokehold.

"You turned into such a whore, fucking everything with a dick then you have the nerve to ask what is wrong with me. You fucking bitch. Your whoring ass gave me HIV."

I felt a pain in my chest from the weight of his words, coupled with the adrenaline pumping through my body and the inability to breathe properly from his firm grip. I began gasping for air.

"Leave her alone….Please stop…" Saphire screamed. Tiffany then ran towards Mikey, hitting him as hard as she could. He released me, and I fell to the floor in tears. I was so overwhelmed with emotions, I could hardly formulate sentences. I wanted to defend myself and tell him the truth about the possible source of his infection but I couldn't. My body wouldn't allow me. Instead, I sat on the floor breathing heavily.

"Mikey, leave her alone, you may hurt the baby." Tiffany said tugging at his arm.

I felt my heart flutter from the look on his face.

"What did you say, he looked at her then back at me, with a look of pure evil that was even scaring me. I had never seen him like this before. It was as if someone had released a demon in him."

Tears streamed down my face, then I found myself

hyperventilating.

"If I can't have you, no one else will." He pulled his gun and Tiffany ran.

"Please don't do this..." I heard Saphire saying in between sobs.

"Please don't hurt her or any of us...Please," Tiffany chimed in.

Next thing I knew, he fired a shot and I felt the most excruciating pain in my abdomen. I clutched my belly and curled up in a ball as I watched blood seeping through my fingers. I cried out in agony. I heard another gunshot which was immediately followed by a sting in my leg. My body suddenly felt numb. I felt like everything was slowing down. I could hear screams and shuffling across the room but in terribly slow motion. I now heard sirens. I heard more gunshots. My vision blurred. A figure fell on the floor next to me with light emanating from it. It had a masculine presence but no distinct facial features. Just light rays shining all around him. I saw more figures surrounding the man and myself but no faces. Everything became a blur. There was now silence.

****

"Even though I walk through the valley of the shadow of death, I will fear no evil. Carry me soft and gentle dear Lord into sleeps arms and beyond. Ease the loneliness of my friends and loved ones I may leave behind as I step bravely in whatever is to follow. Take me Lord but not my child, in Jesus name. Amen"

www.ingramcontent.com/pod-product-compliance
Lightning Source LLC
Chambersburg PA
CBHW060128260626
47160CB00005B/2045